In Strange Waters

An **O'Ceagan's Saga** Novel

Lillian I Wolfe

Published by

Reno, Nevada

ISBN-13: 978-1-942622-20-8

First Edition: January 2019
Lillian I. Wolfe

Front Cover Art by SelfPubBookCovers.com/ mad-moth

Dedication

With love and thanks to Patricia, my best friend and companion of forty years. "Britain is fine in '79" we agreed when she moved in with me to save money for the trip to the World Science Fiction Convention in Brighton, England. She never moved out although we upgraded houses two more times. Thank you for all the encouragement and companionship for these four decades.

About This Book

In Strange Waters is set in the *O'Ceagan's Saga* universe and while some of the main characters from *O'Ceagan's Legacy* appear in the tale, the story is actually about Dari, the *puca* (pooka), and how he is adapting to life on Erinnua. As before, I've kept the characters with a strong Irish influence and speculated quite a bit on what a puca might think or do.

The story builds more on the long relationship between Dari and Sheilan, the *bean sidhe* (banshee), two spirits now living on a world far away from their homeland.

I hope you will enjoy this fanciful tale. If you do like it, please consider leaving a review at whichever marketplace you acquired a copy. Reviews are manna from Heaven for an independent writer, so it would mean a great deal to me as well as possibly pointing other readers toward it.

Contents

Chapter 1

A New World to Explore

Peeking through a break in concealing growth of something resembling an Earth shrub, Dari n'a dearga sniffed the off-putting alien order of the plant and concluded it didn't smell like the ones he knew. From what he'd seen and sniffed so far on this new world he was beginning calling home, none of vegetation did.

But for now, he heard girlish giggles growing louder as his marks made their way down the dirt path that ran through the forest toward the town just on the other side. Chattering as they walked, the pair of young voices carried the same conversation he'd heard thousands of girls utter over the centuries. Boys. It was always about boys with the young lasses. Although for a period there, they'd talked about other girls almost as much. In this sense, life with the humans on Erinnua resembled life back in Ireland.

For this encounter, he'd chosen his young lad form, one that he'd taken from a mid-teen boy back in the eighth century. When the boy had charmed him with his attitude and bravado against a puca, he'd spared his life but taken enough of his flesh to record the form. In this guise, he presented a handsome face dusted with a sprinkling of freckles and capped with dark, reddish-brown hair. Those features always proved attractive to young ladies.

As the girls drew near, he stepped out on the pathway and

strolled toward them, looking as if he had been approaching all along. Giving them a big grin that made his sea-blue eyes sparkle, he greeted them with charm and enthusiasm. "Bedad, if it isn't two of the loveliest colleens I am having the pleasure to see on this stroll. 'Tis just my good fortune to be on the same path this glorious day."

True to form, the lasses giggled, and the ginger-haired girl blushed, coloring her cheeks a fetching dark pink. The other girl, a saucy-looking blond, maintained her composure a little better but smiled back at him. Just beginning to bud out, the rounded bumps on her chest pushed out against her blouse like an inviting pair of small oranges. Not that Dari cared much about that sort of thing, not even in this form.

"You speak rather oddly," she said, a look of curiosity in her huge gray eyes. "You're not from around here, are you?"

He shook his head. "Nay, I have only just arrived in the past few days, and I am still trying to find me way around the area. My name is Dari."

"Well, welcome to the area then. I'm Katy, and this is Maureen." She indicated the shy redhead, who peered more at the ground that at him. "Do you live near here, Dari?"

"I do. Fairly close."

"Then are you enrolled at the town study hall? We've just come from there." She indicated an electronic tablet that she held in her hand as if it explained the whole thing.

"Study hall? Is that like a school or something?" he asked, perplexed by the question.

"Don't you have them where you came from?" Maureen asked, a look of surprise crossing her face along with another blush.

"Well, there were schools and home education and all that,"

he replied. "But I didn't go."

"You didn't?" Katy asked. "But why not?"

"Because," he replied with a wicked laugh, "I am already more educated than you will ever be." With that, his laugh grew into a sound that sounded more like a whinny, and he vanished into thin air.

Shocked, the girls shrieked and ran down the path as fast as they could as the now invisible puca's laugh lingered in the air.

Well, those two will have a fine story to tell their friends, he thought, satisfied with his little prank. 'Twas his first encounter with the humans on the planet. To be honest, he wasn't sure if they even knew what he was.

Back in Ireland, everyone still knew about pucas, but here in a world millions of miles from Earth, he wasn't sure the people even knew much about the old legends let alone his kind. He'd come to the planet with the bean sidhe, Sheilan, on a cargo ship, the Mo Croidhe, that happened to be owned by the very family she had been seeking. While the two of them might have the means to return to Ireland using soil travel, they hadn't tried it out yet. Immortal or not, they were both a little hesitant to trust the travel over such a long distance, and neither was keen to end up stuck in the ether between worlds.

But soon, he would like to return to make sure he could get back and to visit some of his puca friends to boast a bit. Then he worried for a moment or two that if he traveled through, would he be able to return again through the soil connection? It was more complicated than his puca brain could handle.

Materializing back into a corporeal form as a white Irish Hobby pony, Dari wandered farther down the path in the direction the girls had fled. While the pony was a splendid form in Ireland, he'd quickly learned that horses were non-existent on

Erinnua. Either they didn't survive the new land, or the settlers didn't bring them with them.

From what he'd seen, only a few life forms from Earth seemed to thrive here. He'd seen something that resembled a badger, a fox, a couple of rats, and a whole bunch of odd-looking animals that might have been native to the planet. One, in particular, looked like a boar, only much larger with a bluish coat and a longer snout, plus two wicked-looking horns at the side of its head. Grunting a warning at him, the beast dashed away before Dari could study it for long.

To tell the truth, he didn't think this New Ireland felt much like the old sod even though it flourished with lush vegetation enough to remind him of the green hills. Little by little, even the purplish tinted colors on the planet looked more normal to him. But the smell and the taste lacked a great deal of the fresh, sweetness of home.

As he drew near the town, he left the path and made his way to the edge of the forest where he could get a good view. A decent-sized place with dozens of buildings and streets, the town was larger than many of the villages back home but much smaller than a city. He wondered what people called it and how friendly and Irish-like these immigrants might be. Would they be good storytellers or drinking companions? Would they gather at the pub for an evening of song? Along with missing his companions, he also missed the way of life. Maybe later he'd change back to his youth visage and explore, but for now, he wanted to go somewhere else.

The swimming-pool-sized, roughly oval, pond had attracted his attention a couple of days earlier, which brought him back to study it some more. So far, he'd found the water to be different from Earth's, a little bitter to his taste, and it felt heavier and harder to move in. He'd only waded in once, so he thought he'd try again in his horse form. While he had a water-horse-body option as well, he felt the pond wasn't deep enough for him to use it.

Dari stepped into the water, feeling the cool liquid around his legs as his hooves sank into the gritty sand at the bottom. This much felt familiar although still a bit sluggish as he moved through it. He waded out as the water got deeper until he was submerged to almost the top of his back and the liquid sloshed against him. Apart from the color being more purple than blue, the heaviness, and that bitter taste, the liquid surrounding him resembled Earth's lakes. For all that, he observed that the pond seemed to have no life in it apart from a few types of odd-looking vegetation that he couldn't identify as anything that resembled water weeds back home.

He ducked his head below the water, seeing a yellow and red plant with paddles on the end that almost looked like a cactus, but lacking any mouth-injuring thorns. He nudged it with his nose then took a tentative bite and spat it out almost immediately. Extremely bitter and nasty. The horse side did not approve. A fern-looking plant waved at him as the water rolled against it, and he tried a bite of one of the tips.

Popping his head back out, he sputtered and dropped the clump of mushy, icky stuff back into the pond. No wonder no fish swam in the water here. Everything in it tasted terrible.

Wait. What was that?

Out of his horsey eye, he spotted a dart of movement near the fern things and ducked his head back underneath. A little cluster of small triangular fish darted around the ferns, then scurried back into them. Barely larger than tadpoles, they seemed to have only one eye in the middle of their bodies. Peculiar, but at least, indicative of some kind of life.

Wading back out, he trod his way to the top of the rise and gazed out toward the sea. Just below him, the O'Ceagan estate, a large farm where Sheilan's family lived, spread out for miles. For their help on the ship when space pirates with the intent of stealing the cargo nearly destroyed it, the O'Ceagan had given the bean sidhe a small parcel of land near the place where Dari now stood.

Here, Sheilan had mixed the dirt of home that was their portal back to both Ireland and their own world in with the soil of this land. The ban sidhe wasn't actually a family member but had been assigned to the O'Ceagan family many centuries earlier. When the last earth-bound O'Ceagan had died, he and Sheilan had found passage on a ship bound for Erinnua where the rest of the clan had migrated. As fate would have it, the very vessel they'd taken had belonged to the same family.

In many ways, the view reminded the puca of the one from the Wicklow Mountains to the Irish Sea, but the colors were off a tad bit. The result of the red sun, Sheilan told him, but he didn't quite understand it. Nonetheless, the sea here appeared more lavender than blue while the sky carried a deeper, more intense blue-green shade than on Earth. Even though the sun might be red, the beams bursting from it seemed as golden white as the one they'd left.

Curiosity made him wonder about the sea, and if it tasted as bitter as the pond, or if it was salty. Did any life forms swim in the deeper water? Seaweeds? Fish of any sort?

Drawn to it, Dari lazily walked down the slope, picking out the easy way to the shoreline. He stood at the edge for a few minutes letting the waves lap against his hooves, his spirit feeling the call of the sea. Too much time had passed since he'd felt the ocean waves over his water horse body, the initial corporeal form he'd taken on Earth.

Tossing caution to the wind, as was his nature, he trotted into the oncoming waves and dove into them, changing form in the middle of a large swell and becoming the water creature. As a water horse, he was magnificent, nearly eight-feet long from the top of his horse head and mane to the tip of his strong fishtail that propelled him through the water. Long ago, when sailors spoke of sea monsters, they could very well have referred to a puca in water horse form. His powerful body shimmered a cream color as he flipped his sea green fins and tail. His seaweed-looking mane floated back away from his yellow fish-like eyes. Underwater, he could see with more clarity than his horse form could.

As far as Dari knew, he'd always been an energy creature and shapeshifter, who possessed the ability to pull the molecules from surrounding life and transform it into the body he chose. The only thing he needed to create a life form was a sampling of the being, such as the young lad or the Irish pony, in order to manifest it, but it seemed to him, he'd always known the water horse form. Then again, that was so long ago that maybe he just didn't recall acquiring it.

Now he plunged eagerly into the seawater, still feeling the weightier tug of it, but not concerned about it. Perhaps the composition was a little different, but over time he'd get used to it.

More interesting to him was the lack of much life below the waves. He did spot some vegetation growing, but it looked peculiar. More angular than earth's coral, it looked like crystals growing together that sparkled with the sunlight filtering through the water. Then he glimpsed movement from an aquatic creature that shot past him and vanished into the crystals. The fish, if he could call it that, had a single crystal-looking eye and a sharply triangular body with a flat, squished-looking head of the same shape.

As he swam on, he discovered more of the odd sea creatures, all of them looking as if they'd emerged from a Picasso painting. It didn't seem natural, and he thought it strange that life here would evolve like that.

About to turn back toward shore, he noticed a confrontation near a large underwater boulder, and being nosy, decided to investigate. Ahead a large oblong creature bearing ten tentacles grabbed at a smaller animal that resembled a seahorse, but with more dragon-like features. The tail of the sea dragon whipped toward the appendages, knocking them back and trying to break free of one of two that managed to grip it around the waist. The sea dragon used its powerful forearms to pop the central core of the monster, but with as many arms as the squid-like beast had, the dragon's fight looked like a losing situation.

Dari perceived the desperation in the sea dragon's faceted eyes, and he could practically hear the frantic screams from the animal's mind. In his own reckoning, the dragon form appeared similar to him, an underwater mammal with a powerful tail. In the sea dragon's case, a seal-like tail that it now brought around to pound the squid-like beast until it broke two of the tentacles that tried to grip it.

Without another thought, Dari plunged toward the fray and dug in, using his front horse legs to attack.

CHAPTER 2

The Sea Dragon

Swiveling his body around, Dari whipped his tail up to slap one of the creature's long arms away as it tried to make a grab for him. In an instant, the squid thing thrust another tentacle forward, looping it around Dari's neck.

Jerking as daggers of pain shot through his body, he realized the tentacles bore stingers along the bottom. Nonetheless, he'd fought squids and octopuses before; he knew how to avoid the appendages and where to strike with his legs and tail. Mustering his strength, he lashed out with his powerful tail and slammed it against the base of the tentacle as hard as he could. Like a piece of fragile coral, the limb broke off, and Dari shoved himself away as the unattached arm fell off of his neck. Yellow liquid he presumed to be blood oozed from the broken appendage.

Meanwhile, the sea dragon swam to the opposite side to attack the beast from a different direction. It spun to one side and whipped a powerful appendage of its own toward its adversary, catching two more of the tentacles and wrapping around them in a disabling grip, then the dragon pulled back, yanking the squid away from the purchase it had on a boulder.

The damaged body leaped forward as the cephalopod went on the attack against the sea dragon, and in a second, the latter switched to defense mode as it yanked the tentacles hard, breaking two more of them away from the elongated body.

Dari took advantage of the moment and plunged in again, shoving it back and away from the dragon. Taking advantage of the opened space, the dragon brought its own powerful body into a body slam into the squid's core and whirled a spiked tail into the soft body. Yellow and purple liquid burst from the center spreading in a curved wave as the squid jerked away. With the two against it, the monster retreated, giving up its potential prey.

Dari spun to face the sea dragon, which backed away warily from him. In that moment, as a shimmering reflected from the sunlight through the water against crystalline-looking scales on the body, he marveled at the beautiful creature. A crown of thorny-looking horns on its head added to its already aggressive appearance. In addition to the creature's powerful flipper, it bore another tail tipped with a spiked ball of thorns, similar to ones on its head, that extended a good five feet or more from its body. Two long prehensile appendages, similar to tentacles, floated from just below the sea dragon's shoulders.

Now the creature eyed him, a tilt of its head hinting at the uncertainty it felt toward this newcomer in the water. Using its flippers, it worked itself backward from Dari, keeping a close eye on him. He let himself drift back from it as he paddled with his front legs to maintain position.

He sensed the fear more than he saw it. Confused at first—after all, he'd just helped to fight the beast—he soon realized that the sea dragon had never seen anything like him before. He tipped his head in greeting and tried to send a thought to the creature to offer reassurance.

Much like he communicated with Sheilan when they were in energy form, he used an image to convey friend. A simple picture of linked hands wouldn't work with a creature who had no frame of reference, so he settled on a projection of quiet, gently swaying seaweed harboring a fish.

The sea dragon seemed confused as it twisted its head back and forth, trying to decipher what Dari was doing, but then it pulled back sharply and blew a stream of bubbles through the water toward Dari that struck against him, pushing him farther back. Maybe that didn't work so well, he concluded as he paddled harder to maintain his position.

Unexpectedly, a feeling of gratitude flooded his mind, not an image, but a wave of emotion. He tried to return the sentiment, to reassure it that he meant no harm. He detected fear under the thanks that the creature seemed to send. And he identified a feminine gender in the emotions. Certain the sea dragon was female, he attempted to confirm by projecting an image of her with a smaller version, like an offspring.

After a long few moments, she responded with a family image showing three sea dragons hatching from eggs. They could send pictures, he thought with excitement. They could communicate. She seemed a little confused, and Dari floundered, hard-pressed to come up with images that would mean something to her. All the Earth references conveyed nothing significant here so sending a vision that meant something on another world only stumped her. He wanted to communicate his name but wasn't sure what could have any relevance to her since he didn't know what she called anything in her world.

Emotion came through more strongly from her than images, and he felt her uncertainty at trying to connect with him. He showed her a collage of his world, the green grasses of Ireland and the rocky coast. Instead of reassuring her, it made her more nervous, and she backed away a little farther. She showed him a dark cavern in the water where an image of herself or another sea dragon swam through, then she dipped her head forward in a nod of thanks before she turned and swam rapidly away from him.

Dari tried to call her back, wanting her to stay longer, but he couldn't find any symbol or picture that had any meaning to her, and she simply blocked the images and continued away. Although he tried to follow, she soon lost him in the underwater canyon she darted through. Feeling weary and drained, he gave up, slowing and drifting in the water. His body lacked energy, the fight having drained him, and the squid's stings had taken more of a toll on his body, leaving him feeling sore. He was pretty sure an electrical shock had accompanied those piercing barbs.

Unable to follow the sea dragon, he rose to the surface and drew in a long breath of air before turning to look for the shoreline. His ran his eyes along the horizon as he searched until in the distance, he saw the land rising from the water and going up toward the hilly slopes of the town and the farmland of his new home. He'd come much farther than he'd realized. With a shrug, he released the molecules of his body to return to his energy form.

Back at the plot of land beneath a tree, Dari ducked into the soil. While Sheilan had brought it from the Wicklow Hills, the actual dirt had originally come from their dimension and been transferred to Ireland near Connemara. The sidhe used it to travel between their realm and Earth. And the puca, like Sheilan, came from that higher plane where most of the life existed as energy forms. But they also had functions in the lesser worlds, Sheilan's being to warn the O'Ceagan family of danger and death.

His function had never been precisely defined. A creature of chaos, neither good nor evil, he preferred having fun. He had been known to lure silly people to their death, and he was just as likely to befriend one if he took a liking to him. But mostly, he was a prankster, doing simple things like scaring the young women or teasing a lad with his horse form. That worked well on Earth, but he wasn't sure how it would work in this new world.

For now, Dari simply wanted to recharge his energy in the comforting soil of home and wait for Sheilan to come by.

*****

"I'm telling you the truth, Sheilan," Dari said as he sat in his youthful form next to the sturdy tree a short distance from the plot.

The bean sidhe sat by him, long finely-formed legs tucked under her gown with her silver-white hair flowing freely over her shoulders. She wore her young woman aspect, the one that would turn men's heads and make women jealous at her beauty.

"Oh, I do not doubt it, puca. 'Tis a strange world we have come to and many things are different." She held a small animal in her lap, something she called a kitcoon because it looked a bit like a cross between a cat and a raccoon. Although it was four-legged, it also sported a pair of arm-like appendages that it didn't use to run but applied as humans utilized their hands. At the moment, it had those little paws wrapped around her right hand to hold it while it licked at her fingers.

"The filthy creature stung me," Dari complained, still talking about the squidie thing. "And it hurt and felt like jolts of fire went through my body. It left me feeling drained. What does that to one of our kind?"

"Well, obviously, one of those octopus-like creatures. But take it as a warning, Dari. The life forms on this world are not like the ones we have lived with for centuries. Just because the humans came here, does not mean all life is compatible with them. Look at this little fellow, for instance. He is friendly and likes to be petted like a dog or a cat, but you cannot assume he is like either of them. He has bitten me twice since I befriended him, but he does seem to enjoy the companionship on his terms."

"That sounds like a cat to me." Dari eyed the little animal with suspicion. "And he looks a lot like one. Is it full-grown?"

"No, 'tis a baby, I think. It seems very young. I found it in the woods wandering on its own."

"Anyhow, the sea dragon, as I call her, seemed somewhat friendly, but I couldn't communicate with her very well. Where we can use telepathy, sending images, I could not seem to find the right pictures that she could recognize."

"Perhaps you need to study more about this planet. Learn more about the underwater world and how it functions before you try to use any images to communicate. The sea dragon did understand some, it seems, and she recognized that you were trying to help her. But you look totally alien to her in any form you choose to use. It sounds as if the underwater life here is even more different than the land animals I have encountered." Sheilan scratched the kitcoon under the chin, and the animal made a chortling sound.

"Come walk a bit with me, Dari." The bean sidhe set the little animal on the ground as she rose to her feet. "You stay here, Chaka," she told the kitcoon. In answer, it curled up into a ball at the base of the tree.

"You've named it already?"

"Not really. It is more a variation on the sounds he makes when he's excited." She demonstrated by making a *chak-a-chak-a* noise.

The kitcoon's head snapped toward her, and it responded with a higher-pitched chattering of the cry, then tucked its head back into its body to sleep.

Dari laughed. "Perhaps it thinks you are its mother."

He followed the bean sidhe into the woods a short distance from their small land grant. While the trees were similar to the ones on Earth, their leaves were shaped differently, more rounded and thicker, and the colors tended to yellow-tones with red-looking veins through them.

"The squidie-thing had yellow blood, I think," Dari said as he noted the coloring of the foliage. "And it squirted a purple ink rather than a black one. At least, I think it intentionally squirted it out, but the sea dragon had hit it pretty hard so it could have been something else."

"That is interesting. Most earth animals have red blood because it is iron based. Perhaps some other mineral is the basis of the blood here. Did you notice any smell from it?"

"I was under water. I do not detect scents well under water." He frowned at her. "You know that, do you not?"

"Ah, I forgot. So far, I have not seen the blood of any of the animals I have encountered. It is possible all the life here has yellow blood except for the humans and any of the animals they brought with them, but it would seem that it might make it difficult for them. Then again, they sowed their own food plants, and they seemed to thrive in the land here. Perhaps it is not that much different."

"What animals did they bring with them?" Dari asked with a snort that sounded very horse-like. "From my observation, they didn't seem to bring any horses or cattle."

"True enough. I have seen chickens, ducks, pigs, and sheep. When I asked Grania about it, she told me that several species and none of the fish they brought were able to adapt to Erinnua. They do import some beef and fish from one of the other planets, I understand."

"From what I have witnessed of the underwater life here, in both the sea and the ponds, it is peculiar. Everything I have seen so far is very angular, crystalline, and most only have one eye, placed a little off center, at that. Except for the sea dragon. She had two faceted eyes, and her body shimmered like crystals, but she seemed almost Earth-like." He described her in detail, raving over her colors and the unusual horns that surrounded the top of her head.

"You sound like you are infatuated with her," Sheilan commented with a wry smile. "Is it possible my puca friend may be feeling something romantic toward this creature?"

"What? Are ye daft? I simply find her unique and attractive. And the closest thing to a water horse or any horse that I have found so far."

"Of course, I understand that. 'Tis difficult to not have any of your own kindred around. But we do have each other, Dari, and our kind is not really like any of them."

"True enough. We are sidhe, and we are truly stranded on an alien world."

"Not stranded," Sheilan objected with a dismissing wave of her hand. "Just not rushing to get back to our dimension."

"Are you confident the dirt will work or are you just procrastinating?"

She laughed. "I am reasonably confident the dirt will transport us to Wicklow. I do not know if it will take us to our home, but from Ireland, we can travel there. 'Tis also true that I am procrastinating a bit. I do not want to face the council and tell them what I have done. It was not forbidden, but neither was it implied that a bean sidhe could go off world to pursue the family. As I recall, it created quite a ruckus when the first bean sidhe scooped up some soil and set sail for the new world."

She paused, sighed, and gazed around at the lush forest with its abundant trees and scattered wildlife. "Truth be told, I am more worried that the soil will not transport us back here. I think I formed the link correctly, but until it is tested, I can't be sure."

"So are you saying, I might travel through it to see me friends, but then not be able to return except by taking another spaceship?"

She nodded. "It is a possibility."

"Is there not a way to test it without one of us going through?" He didn't want to be the guinea pig for this, but if it meant never seeing his puca companions again, it might come to it. He suspected Sheilan had far less desire to return than he did. The family she served lived here, and none remained in Ireland to need her. The bean sidhe did not have any ties with others like her. He knew that when he'd chosen to join her, just as he had known there was always a possibility that he wouldn't be able to return home.

"How are you feeling now?" Sheilan asked, changing the subject. "Do you still feel tired and weakened from your encounter with the squidie?"

"Squidie? Good enough name for it, I suppose." Dari shook his head and cast a sheepish smile at her. "No, not so tired anymore although a bit sore. 'Tis odd, to be sure. Not much bothers our immortal energy field and 'tis scary to have something affect you like that. Even piercing through the corporeal construct is rare. It was not like the targassium crystal that weakened us both on the ship coming here in the way that it drained, but it still frightened me some."

"Look," she said pointing to a small clearing between two trees where a tortoise-looking, shell-covered creature with six legs lumbered across the expanse. "It's a range tortoise if I recall what Grania called it correctly."

"Six legs," Dari mumbled. "Do all the creatures here have six legs?"

"No, the spiders have a dozen." She pointed upward to the top of the tree where a red spider the size of a bird perched in a web that resembled a basket. The legs seemed to form a spiky halo around its entire body. It even appeared to have a beak.

"I think it may be possible that creature's ancestor mated with a canary."

She shrugged. "So long as it stays up there. Keep in mind that the waters may have similar life forms. Sadly, I cannot go under the waves with you for more than a short distance."

He understood. She was limited by her bean sidhe form, which only allowed her to shift to a few human-like shapes: the young woman, a maiden, and an old crone being among them. She could alter the woman some, changing hair or eye color and adding to the features, but when she was called, it was one of the predetermined shapes that appeared.

"Be cautious if you continue to explore the waters, Dari. Remember that this is a totally different world despite the similarities. Until we know the nature of the planet, we will not be at ease in the setting."

The puca nodded his agreement. He would definitely exercise caution as he explored. Sheilan turned back toward the knoll where she'd left her new companion, and Dari continued on toward the town.

As he walked, he thought, Perhaps I'll find some clues in the town on how to communicate with the sea dragon better. Then again, would the creature be familiar with any of the human objects?

CHAPTER 3

Playing Pranks

In his pony form, Dari paced at the edge of a lake, his steps slow and relaxed as he studied the water. As lakes went, it appeared about the size of Lake Owel back in Ireland, twice as long as it was wide, and judging by the colors across it, he thought it might vary quite a bit in depth. The overcast sky made the lavender shading to the water less predominant, so it looked more like the gray-blue water he was used to seeing.

Taking a deep breath, he decided to take the plunge, metaphorically speaking, and eased his forelegs into the liquid. It felt cool, but not too chilly, as it lapped against his skin, so he walked into it until the water reached past his shoulders, tickling at his neck. Ducking his head under, he peered around him to get an idea of what might lie ahead.

In just a few more paces, he could see that the land sloped downward at a shallow angle, leading him to deeper water. Around him, he noticed stones and, hidden amongst them, similarly-sized shell animals that moved very little, except where a few shifted with the water movement away from his hooves. Not too unlike the clams and oysters of Earth. He walked a little farther forward before leaping from the water and transforming in mid-air into the water horse.

Diving back into the water head first, Dari turned toward the deeper water and swam ahead. Again, he didn't see as much underwater vegetation as he would have expected but spotted considerably more than had been in either the pond or the last lake he'd checked out. He swam on, glimpsing the peculiar triangular creatures that he'd noticed in the ponds. Not fish, at least not in the sense he knew, but an underwater inhabitant of every pond and stream he'd checked out, they grew bigger in the lake environment with these being at least a two-hand spread in width.

As he swam deeper, less of the clouded sunlight filtered through and he had to rely on his underwater vision to see the larger boulders and crevices in the submerged landscape. A mass of colorful creatures clinging to a tall, column-looking rock caught his attention, so he maneuvered toward it. Comparing it to a coral reef with mollusks covering it, he noted that like so much of the sea life here, crystalline scales of varying hues of blue, yellow, and green covered their angular bodies.

A ragged opening in the rock drew his eyes, and Dari navigated closer to investigate. Just as he started to peer into the dark hole, a sea creature darted out of it. Dari jerked back, barely getting out of the way in time, and backpedaled if you could call the reverse flipping of his tail that, as he looked at the very long sea snake that spun its body into a circle. While the purple body, accented with a line of small yellow dots down it, registered in Dari's mind, other features caught his immediate attention. Like the sea dragon, two whip-like appendages, a few inches back from the head, bore stingers or barbs on the ends and swayed around as the creature moved. At the opposite end, the tail ended with one of the spiked paddles. More to his dismay, Dari realized that the snake seemed to be winding up for a strike at him.

As the snake shot forward and the tendrils by its head spun

toward him, the puca transformed, his glowing gold energy ball shooting to the surface a split second before the tendrils would have grabbed him. Above the water, the energy form darted for the shore. As he landed on the sand, Dari switched to his young lad form and collapsed in a heap.

He felt drained just from the escape and the third transformation of the morning. In fact, he didn't feel entirely whole, as if he couldn't pull enough molecules to create the body. Using his elbows, he pulled himself up the sandy bank to the grassy edge. Aware of the gritty feel of the sand, Dari realized that he was naked, and he hoped no young lasses came his way any time soon. At the moment, he didn't have the energy to clothe himself or to shift forms again.

He closed his eyes and contemplated the latest developments. A deadly-looking sea snake, a murderous squidie, and an equally ferocious sea dragon so far. What else lived under the water that could threaten him? He didn't mind a good fight, but he did want to steer clear of those painful barbs. The triangular water inhabitants appeared harmless and ignored him, but those larger creatures seemed more territorial.

It presented a dilemma for him. As a puca, the water horse was his prime form. He'd used it many times to lure victims into the water when he felt particularly ornery. After a few centuries of drowning foolish and drunk victims, he'd grown somewhat tired of the sport and found it more entertaining to merely frighten them. But he feared he had no way to effectively defend against the underwater lords who felt threatened by a lowly pony.

*****

Sitting at an outdoor table at a tea shop in the town, Dari and

Sheilan had tea with biscuits while he told her about the morning's escapade. She chuckled, finding his distress amusing, something that annoyed him. "'Tis not funny! The damnable snake could have killed me."

She arched an eyebrow. "Killed you? Really? Are you not immortal, Dari na'deargh? Maybe stunned you, killed the water horse body, but not the sidhe."

He took a gulp, savoring the sweetness of the berry tea, glad for the reassuring warmth and flavor of the beverage. While he didn't need the sustenance from human food, his corporeal body could absorb it, and he found comfort in the custom.

"Do you believe that to be true? Has no sidhe ever been permanently destroyed?" These were heavy thoughts for the puca, who had seldom worried about such things.

Sheilan cast an indulgent look at him. "None that I've ever heard of, let alone witnessed. I do know that a construct can be killed, but the energy form is released when it happens and that form, which is the true sidhe, survives. Granted, the death you might suffer could be painful and even a little traumatic, but it won't be permanent."

He sniffed at a tea cake, smelling a bit of clove or something similar in it, then took a bite. He chewed a few times, then said, "I would that I felt as sure of this as you do, Sheilan. On the ship here, I had been certain that I was dying when we encountered the raw power crystal. It felt like it could snuff out my life force completely. Did you not feel it as well?"

"Aye, I did. 'T'was powerful, to be sure, and something we both feared, but it did no permanent harm. I do not believe it would have destroyed us completely though." She paused, raised her eyes to meet his. "You know, the humans claim to have a soul, something bestowed by their god. And they believe the soul is indestructible, that even when their corporeal form dies, the soul continues. Now where it might go, I do not know, and I do not believe they are even sure of it. But the point is that they do believe it goes on. Now, our own energy form may be similar to this soul, only more advanced. We still retain memory, communicate, and travel in an energy ball."

Dari thought he understood what she meant, but it still troubled him. "I hope you are right, for if I am to continue to explore the waters here, I fear I might find out first hand if it is true."

"Are you still thinking about your sea dragon-lass?" she asked, her question cutting to the core of his thoughts.

"I confess I am. Not that she is mine in particular, mind you. But she is the closest creature I have encountered so far to my water horse. Would it not be fun to cultivate a friendship with a similar animal on this planet?"

"Ah, my friendship is not enough," she sighed in mock distress.

"'Tis excellent, of course, Sheilan. But I would enjoy an underwater companion. You are similar to the humans here, and you seem to have forged a connection with young Grania, so why should I not seek more companionship as well?"

Nodding, she said, "While that is true, and I am enjoying actually talking once more with a human, the truth is that one day, I will have to face her in my base form again and call her to the grave. Then I can but hope that the humans are correct about their soul survival."

She looked sad, and Dari recalled that she had already faced Grania twice before when the ship was in danger on the trip from Earth. Fortunately, the disaster was averted, and they all arrived here safely.

"Where is the captain now?" he asked.

"On the space station to oversee the repairs on her ship. She said that she wishes to be certain everything is done properly. But back to your problem. Have you tried again to contact the dragon fish?"

"Sea dragon," he corrected at once. "I have not gone back in the sea if that is what you're asking. And telepathy does not seem to work well from a distance. In fact, it was hard enough with her. I still need to find images to convey thoughts to her. We can exchange emotions, but they are not specific enough."

"Did you try the library building? Humans keep a lot of information there so if they have explored the sea, then you might find clues."

"'Tis odd, but I am not seeing any indication of humans exploring the waters, or even much using them, around here. Back in Ireland, there would be human debris and trash on the bottom of the lakes and oceans. The streams would remain clear and even some of the ponds, but there would be some indication that they had been in the water. I am wondering if they just avoid them here."

"Perhaps I can ask Grania when I see her next. Or maybe you can ask one of those young lasses who keep eyeing you." She tilted her head toward a table next to the street where a trio of teenage girls glanced furtively at him and giggled. "Seems to me there's plenty of the local life who might like to be your friends."

He squirmed a bit under their attention and frowned. "I don't know about that, Sheilan. I cannot be sure if I can trust meself with humans. Why do they always giggle?"

"Be brave, puca," Sheilan said as she paid for their tea and left him to face the girls alone.

Seeking the distraction, Dari sauntered over to introduce

himself, telling them he had only recently come to the town. They invited him to sit, so he did and soon chatted with the girls, learning that they all attended a school in the village and were in the second level, whatever that meant. He nodded as if he understood and kept talking. Sure, they were like the lasses back in Ireland. They even had the same accent, although they used a few words he'd not heard before. Then again, he had some words they'd not heard, like Tommyknockers, culchie, selkie, and puca, to name a few. Words that were still used back home, but apparently didn't migrate with the settlers. Of course, he was most disturbed that they'd not heard puca before and had no idea what it was.

"Well, darlings, here is what you need to know about a puca. He's a sidhe, one of the faery folk, if you know what I mean."

"Faery folk," Abby exclaimed. Her dark brown eyes growing wider and then she giggled. "There's no such thing. Are you telling a story, boy?"

"'Tis no story," he said, his mouth drawing a little sullen. "In Ireland, the sidhe are real enough, and the people would be wise to respect them. In fact, they often leave food or drink for them by the old wells and sacred places."

"Of course, they do," Edith agreed. A petite blond girl with an infectious grin, she made an awkward sign of the cross on her chest, then blinked her dark blue eyes at him. "And most likely some animal comes by during the night and eats it, so they call him one of these she-things."

"When you say 'she', are you referring to a female?" This came from Megan, a button-nosed brunette with flashing green eyes. "Are all the faeries female?"

Dari shook his head sharply and spelled it out. "They are not all female or male. In fact, some have no gender; they just are.

People used to respect them more." He stared at the pavement below his feet. For all that this looked and sounded like the place he'd left behind, he realized significant differences existed here. If the people of Ireland were showing a lack of respect for the old spirits of the land, the people of Erinnua didn't even know about them. His mouth tightened.

"How do you know so much about them anyway?" Megan asked. "Did you study up on Earth or something?"

"Or something. Let me tell you a thing or two. 'Tis not wise to mock a faery. They have powers humans don't have."

"Such as?" Abby prompted.

"Such as the ability to change appearances and to travel quickly from one point to another practically undetected. One of them even warns people of death."

That brought a few snickers and an outright giggling laugh.

"Or, there is a trickster of sorts," he said in a low voice. "'Tis called a puca, and it can take several forms, but the most common one is a large white horse with red eyes. And that horse can kill a human with his hooves or bite them with his teeth. It might even lure the unsuspecting human onto its back for a ride, then throw him into a lake to drown."

Their eyes widened as he talked.

Then… breaking the mood entirely, Edith asked, "What's a horse?"

Dari loosed a heavy sigh. These children knew nothing about Earth's tales or even what a horse was. Of course not, they'd never seen one. With a sigh of resignation, he replied, "A horse is a big four-legged animal that trots on all its legs, stands taller than Megan, or me, for that matter. It has a large head with a long snout…" He used his hands to try to convey the shape of the face. "Quite a magnificent-looking creature, it is, and most times, they are useful to people. But the puca is not a true horse. The puca is a shape-shifting spirit. And most times, he is a prankster and plays tricks on foolish humans."

The girls laughed again, not taking him seriously at all.

"You're a good storyteller, Dari," Abby said between laughs as she gasped for air.

"I'm a good game player also," he replied. "How about we play hide-and-seek? I'll go hide in those bushes over there, and you can come to seek me. If you find me, then I'll give you a treat. But if you don't find me, then you owe me a story in return."

"Deal," Megan said, nudging her friends. "We'll hide our eyes and count to fifty, then come looking for you. Bet we find you within five minutes."

As soon as they turned their backs to him and covered their eyes with their hands, Dari made for the bushes, removed his clothes, hid them, and released his physical form. Then he waited. Soon the girls came and searched for him.

Abby found his pants and held them up to her friends. "Oh, my gawd, do you suppose he's naked?"

"Let's find him quickly then," Megan whispered with a touch of wickedness.

They searched high and low through the bushes, around the bushes, and in the nearby area, but of course, they didn't find him. When they'd gone quite a ways looking for him, Dari took on his youthful form again, pulling on his clothes and feeling relieved that they hadn't taken his britches with them. Then he went back to the table at the café and waited for them to return.

Edith saw him first and nudged Megan, pointing to him. He waved cheerfully and grinned as they approached him.

"How did you do that?" Abby asked. "We looked everywhere and even found your pants. We should have kept them, I see."

He wiggled an eyebrow at them. "I reckon I am just better at the game than you are. Now you owe me a story."

As they sat down, Megan asked, "About what? Anything in particular?"

"Tell me a story about the seas here. One with sailors and shipwrecks. Do you know any of those?"

The girls cast uncomfortable looks at each other until Abby spoke. "We don't have those kinds of stories. No one goes out on the sea or the lakes. Not since the first arrivals on Erinnua. They're considered dangerous, and the home to monsters. Even fish don't live in the waters of the ponds."

Edit cleared her throat nervously. "I heard that a man once went out on Loch Cullen, and he never came back. He'd made a wee boat and took it out, but both he and the boat disappeared."

"You're telling me that no one has ever explored under the water in the oceans or the lakes?"

"It's forbidden," Megan said in a low voice. "No one is allowed to go into the waters. Rumors say that even the water is dangerous to humans. We're never to drink any of it."

Stunned by this, Dari asked, "What do you do for drinkin' water and to make beverages?"

"The early settlers built purification plants to take the fresh lake water and clean it up so we can use it. The plants provide enough water for our small population," Megan answered.

"Didn't you learn this in school?" Abby asked, a frown making a furrow between her eyes.

Dari realized his questions made him suspicious and decided not to pursue it anymore. "I did not go to school here. In fact, 'tis only been a few days that I've been here."

"You're from off-world," Edith said, sitting up straight and nearly clapping her hands together. "How exciting. Where are you from and what's it like? Was it Cardyff?"

He shook his head. "No, not this star system at all. I need to go now."

He sprang to his feet and gave them a little half bow before pivoting and heading for the road that would lead back to the O'Ceagan farm. As he briskly walked away, he heard the scrape of chairs and knew that the girls would follow him to see where he went. A sly smile and red-tinged twinkle in his eyes transformed his face to something decidedly wicked.

Picking up his pace, he took the road into the woods, then stepped off the path and changed into his full draft horse stallion aspect, the one that was huge and would both entice and frighten most humans. Like silver-white threads, his long mane and tail draped in elegant waves, but his red, glowing eyes remained his most striking feature. As Dari waited for the girls to come close, he could hear them chattering.

Choosing his moment, he sprang from the woods onto the path just in front of them. Rearing up, the spirit horse whinnied loudly and punched his front legs in the air as if boxing another horse.

Edith shrieked, turned, and started running. A moment later, Abby followed her. Megan lingered a little longer, slowly backing away from him. "A horse," she whispered, then Dari dropped his legs to the ground with the full force of his body on them making a loud, powerful thud that sent dirt flying from the path.

That did it. Megan shrieked, pivoted and ran. He whinnied again, then set off running after her, catching up with little effort and trotting beside her, his huge horse body thudding. The girl looked panicked and tried to run faster. Apparently not seeing a piece of wood in the path, she stumbled over it, falling to the ground. As she pulled to her knees, staring into his face, he blew his hot breath over her.

"Please don't hurt me," she cried, tears forming in her frightened eyes. "I mean you no harm." Her words caught as she repeated them over and over.

Dari leaned forward, caught the green ribbon from her hair and pulled on it, yanking it loose. Megan screamed.

Satisfied with his work and his prize, Dari trotted off leaving the sobbing girl in the middle of the road.

CHAPTER 4

Establishing Communication

Seawater washed against the shore, the waves tickling over Dari's toes. He wiggled them, feeling the familiar touch of a welcoming environment, the feeling of home. He plunged into the waves, his human form embracing the wet splashes as he swam away from the shore. Even though the water chilled him, he relished its refreshing and cleansing silky caress against his naked body,.

As he swam farther out, his human body strained to push through the water until, in the swell of another wave, he transformed and the water horse plunged beneath the crest to the wonders of the world below. Joy surging through him, Dari swam amongst the abundant and colorful underwater life – schools of bluefish, a growth of long, waving seaweed, mussels, prawns, and so much more. And there, just a short distance away, a fellow puca water horse flipped his tail in greeting, and he darted toward it to play.

A nudge against his cheek snapped Dari out of his daydream to find himself nose to nose with a cat-like face peering at him. The kitcoon poked a stubby digit into his shoulder and chittered with the noise that matched its name. The puca sat up and looked around, spotting Sheilan a few yards down the beach. He waved at her, catching her eye.

She picked up her pace as she came closer to him and called out, "If I did not know better, I would have thought you were sleeping. But that isn't possible, is it?"

He climbed to his feet, brushing the sand from his clothes. "No, 'tis not. However, me mind did wander a tad. I was recalling the Irish Sea on Earth and how much life it has." He paused to gaze at the purple-hued waters and sighed. "To be frank, the waters here are practically barren. Not much life in them at all, and what is there is strange. You would think there would be a lot more."

"Have you tried to contact her again?" Sheilan took a step into the edge of the water, letting it brush against her bare foot.

"I did try, not long ago. I sent images of various things I thought might have meaning to her, but I had no response. Not even a sense of her presence."

Sheilan pulled her foot back and turned to stand by him. "It feels different. You are right about that. The composition is not exactly as 'tis on Earth. Perhaps the sea is younger, and the water life is still adapting or else it is older and dying. Or –" She paused and frowned as if a new thought had occurred to her.

"Or what?"

"Or the humans have interfered in its development."

"No. I do not think so. The *cailíns* I talked to said that humans were forbidden from going into the water."

"Forbidden? Now why would that be, I wonder?" Her lips broke into a half-smile. "Those young girls told you that, you say?"

At his nod, she went on. "Just to satisfy me curiosity, did you, by chance, show them your true nature?"

"Ah, what do mean by that?" Dari replied.

She laughed. "I mean, my old friend, that I heard gossip this afternoon of three girls frightened by a huge white beast they called a har-ise. Would that have anything to do with you?"

He kicked at the sand, not looking at her. "Well, they had no idea what a puca is or you or any other of the sidhe, so I thought they needed a little education."

Her laughter grew and rang out over the sea. "Maybe that is a good thing, Dari. But you had best not get too cocky. So, tell me the truth now. Why do you wish to find the sea dragon so much?"

He crossed his arms over his chest and gazed across the water. "When you came up, my daydream included one of my companions, another puca, and I was playing chase with him underwater. An energy being I might be, but my water form is the one I love best. I miss those moments with others like me. If I am stuck here, then the sea dragon comes closest to being like me. I would like to befriend her and perhaps one day race around the water with her."

"So you are lonely for your own kind and, as the humans call it, you are homesick. One day soon, one of us will need to try the soil travel to Earth. Once we establish that it works, then you can visit whenever you want." She reached down and picked up Chaka, cuddling the animal in her arms. "As for now, you just keep working on the connection, and remember that we spent a good long time finding common symbols to communicate when we first met."

She started to walk away, but stopped and turned back to him. "And one more thing, puca. You have more options in the forms you can take than I do. Perhaps you should create a new one."

"Perhaps," he said and turned back to the sea. Time to go for a swim.

The sea seemed darker than the last time he'd gone in, but

then some clouds had moved in bringing rain. He barely noticed the drops cutting into the surface, although the water seemed rougher and harder to swim through. Once he went a little lower, it calmed somewhat although the heaviness of the water remained. He couldn't help thinking about what Megan had said about the water being dangerous. Could whatever was deadly to the humans affect his water horse form?

Concentrate, he reminded himself. He needed to focus on finding the sea dragon and sending images to her. Following the remembered path he'd taken to where he'd encountered her facing off against the squidie, he looked for any outcroppings or boulders that matched his memory and made more than a couple of wrong turns before he found one that looked right. When he felt confident he was close, he tried to contact her again.

Forming an image in his mind of the incident, he projected it out and hoped he had the right path to her subconscious. When they had connected and sent images before, he registered the frequency, for lack of a better term, that her mind used. For now, he could only send and hope that she received and responded to him. He showed her fighting the squidie and him coming to aid her. As he tried to demonstrate he was a friend, he sent calm and friendly feelings to her since the emotion had transferred before.

Getting nothing, he repeated it another two times as he swam a little farther along, hoping that he still followed the path she took. Ahead he spotted a family of one-eyed angle-crabs darting across the sand to a cluster of shiny, crystalline seaweed where they scuttled in, disappearing among the strands. A moment later, a fish-sized creature that looked like a lop-sided wrasse came along, digging its pointed nose into the sand as if sniffing a trail. When it spotted Dari, it paused, turned, and dashed away as fast as it could swim.

Obviously not a great predator, Dari decided, just one that had a fondness for the little angle-crabs and wasn't about to take on the bigger creature in the sea. He supposed that he must seem like a monster to the local sea life, what little there was, and certainly, he was alien to them. He wasn't kidding when he said that the closest underwater life to him was the sea dragon.

But he decided to send the image of the crabs seeking protection and being harbored in the seaweed to the dragon along with the emotions of happiness and comfort. Maybe she would interpret it as safe if she actually received it.

As Dari swam, he recognized a fissure he'd passed while pursuing her and took heart that he might be headed in the right direction. Without warning, an image flashed in his mind, repeating the incident with the squidie, but from the sea dragon's point of view rather than his. She was responding to him by showing him what she saw. Things seemed a little distorted in her eyes, but she did see him with alarm at first until she realized he was trying to help her. But he also detected the suspicion after the squidie had fled and the uncertainty if he was to be trusted or not.

Then she sent something that surprised him. It was a symbol that resembled a question mark. Did she understand and use this common symbol? He sent it back with the more human-looking version. She duplicated it. Then she conveyed an image of two of her kind, small ones, side by side, and darting in the water in play.

He responded with a similar image of two water horses playing in the waves, then the somewhat human symbol of two hands touching, then two paws touching, and finally, two hooves touching. He paused and waited. She returned an image of two dragon hands pressed against each other. Taking a chance, Dari sent a dragon hand tapping a hoof. She repeated it.

Elation rocked his body like a small boat in the water; they were making progress. He showed her the shoreline, and the horse form swimming in it with its head above the water. After a few moments, she sent an image of a domed city underwater, buildings in ruin, and a few sea dragons swimming through it. Was this her home? If so, what had happened? His concern seemed to spook her, and he sensed her alarm before she shut down the image and broke the connection between them.

For another hour, Dari tried to reestablish the connection, pleading with her to come back. But all his efforts proved unsuccessful. Feeling weary and his body more sluggish than it should have been, he decided to give up for the day.

Swimming to the surface, he rolled in the rough sea a long way before he broke to the surface where the rain pounded down into it. With water streaming down his horse face, Dari swiveled his neck around looking for the shore. He barely spotting the rising hills of land in the distance through the downpour. He looked for landmarks to lock his current location in his mind so that he could return to it quickly, then made the switch to his energy form and zipped toward the shore.

In less than five minutes, he'd returned to the shore and changed back into his human form. He grabbed his now soaking wet clothes and pulled them on before heading back to the tree above his and Sheilan's home plot. Bedad, but they needed to do something about making a dry shelter under that tree. Abandoning the clothes again, he released the human form allowing his energy to dart into the less wet shelter of the tree.

*****

With the next day being warm and sunny, Dari trotted down to the seashore, changed to his energy form, and projected himself to the point just above the sea, or at least close to it, where he'd made contact. He didn't switch to the water horse but lingered above the sea as he considered his next move. He figured he'd try to contact her again, but he didn't want to frighten her.

Abruptly an image popped into his thoughts, and he knew at once it came from her. She showed him a large dome with the city in it, only it wasn't ruined. From her, he sensed it once had been like that, and it was beautiful. The dwellings were like high rise condos on Earth with open entries at every level since they could swim to them. Visually, they resembled sheltered caves where they could sleep and rest. Not places where they actually lived as they had no possessions that he could see as she showed him one of the caves. Apparently, a communal species, they stayed in one central location in the water, or so it seemed.

She showed him many of her kind swimming in the area, darting in and out of the caves, then leaving the dome through one of the portals in it. It didn't seem to be built to hold air in it, but to provide protection to them. Curious, he wished for a way to ask her about it – the purpose and how it was built. Did they have a language? If so, and if he could create their form, could he learn their speech? He wanted to know so much more and to be able to talk with her.

Then she showed him something resembling a crude map through the underwater territory that would lead him to the domed city. Could that be an invitation?

Chapter 5

A History Lesson

With the image of the course to the sea dragon's home in his mind, Dari set off in the direction she had sent. He kept his energy form for now so he could move more quickly through the path. He thought he might be able to pop in closer, but he wasn't confident enough on this world to do it. As he progressed, he began to see more underwater life, such as plants and a few tree-sized ones. All of them were angular in shape as if someone had taken the plant and twisted it, and they all shimmered with a crystalline look.

That seemed to frequent here, he thought. From the fish to the shell creatures to the plants, they were misshapen and bore the look of hard glass rather than scales. In fact, any life form he'd seen, except the sea dragons and the squidie, had that in common. It didn't seem to apply to the land creatures since the animals that were native to it looked normal enough apart from their extra pair of limbs.

Dari whirled around a rock and got his first glimpse of the dome ahead. More massive than he'd thought, it rose at least three hundred feet above the seabed and was clear, but cracked in places. Just as he'd seen in the sea dragon's images, the dome had a visible opening, triangular and extending about fifteen feet, he guessed. Beyond was the city if he could term it that. In so many ways, it looked like the worst slum he'd ever seen, even worse than the poorest, most-bombed section of Derry during the troubles.

At this point, he shifted to his water-horse form and progressed forward at a slower pace. Once he drew within a few yards of the dome, he paused to study the scene before him. He spotted a ring made of stone or lava rock, something on the porous side, within the dome. A break, either natural or created, came into view off to his left where the triangular opening led to an entry path through the opening in the stone. Most of the caves facing toward the center of the dome seemed to be geological, but given the symmetry of them, they had to have been constructed or shaped. Many appeared to be crumbling while others were blocked with debris and broken rocks.

Rising higher toward the top of the dome, Dari had a view of the entire colony. Below the towering walls, a large open area filled the center of this section. Perhaps it had been a market or a playground or something similar. Now, he could see six other rings within the dome, all of them with the same basic shape and layout. He swam to the left, starting to circle around the outside of the dome. A mostly clear area of at least fifteen feet separated the dome walls from the ring, but they continued to make giant round circles of dwellings from each entrance he noted as if they were neighborhoods.

Then he came to one section that looked like a bomb had been dropped on it. He'd seen enough of this kind of damage in small areas of Belfast in the mid-twentieth century, by human reckoning. But this was worse than any of that with caves crushed and blackened, supporting walls twisted and burnt-looking. Even the entry to this one had been broken, and it had collapsed to the sea floor. The dome itself sagged like a deflated balloon.

Not liking the feeling of it and sensing danger around it, Dari began to pull away from the section, giving it a wide berth. Whatever happened here had been a complete disaster for the city. A volcano or other earth spewing event? An earthquake, maybe? Did they even have those on this planet?

At that moment, he got an image from the sea dragon showing that she approached and got a distinct feeling he should wait. He slipped to a safe-looking spot where a few of the odd fish were feeding in a weedy growth of some sort. So far, he hadn't encountered anything dangerous, like the squidie or the snake he'd found in the lake. But that didn't mean they might not be watching him and looking for an opportunity to attack a poor unsuspecting water horse. Then again, they didn't know exactly what he was. Would that make them more or less likely to attack?

A few more moments passed, then she swam around the curve, and he moved a little farther toward the dome so she could spot him, then began a slow horse paddle toward her. She stopped about five feet from him, using her tail to balance and hold her position, just as he did. As she tilted her head and torso forward in acknowledgment, he returned the greeting. Dari projected an image of his hoof and her clawed appendage coming together and clasping in friendship. He hoped she interpreted it correctly and didn't see it as an aggressive action.

Her face conveyed a puzzled or uncertain expression, and she sent a question mark image again. He repeated it, wishing for the human form where he could actually clasp one hand in the other to show her what he meant and put a friendly smile on his face at the same time. The horse head could smile, but it sometimes looked more threatening than welcoming.

She hesitated a moment, then propelled herself forward a

little, tentatively offering her clawed hand toward him. Carefully, he brought his right front leg up to present the hoof to her. Tilting her head as she locked her eyes on his, she reached to touch his hard-edged hoof. The claws were like fingernails, but sharper, he thought, more like a cat's claws, but the skin of her hand felt silky as she slid it up his foreleg. He likened it to the feel of a reptilian animal, but with the smoothness of glass scales.

They had made contact, and as nervous as Dari had been over touching her, he found the connection easier than he'd expected. He felt he had nothing to fear from her, but she was the one taking all the risk in this exchange. If he could just talk to her, it would be so much easier, he lamented. As Sheilan had hinted, if he could get a sample of her body's building structure, then he could duplicate a form similar to hers which might allow them to communicate better.

For now, he showed her an image of the severely damaged section of the structure and used the question mark to ask what happened.

After a few moments, she began sending images, like a film, of the dome with the sense this was how it was long ago. Dari could see it as it had been with thousands of the sea dragons and other creatures swimming in one of the neighborhoods. Young ones frolicked among them, little darting sea dragonets that played in the open area. Along the edge of the center, an open-stall market displayed fish, seaweed, foods that looked like vegetables and fruits, and other edibles that the sea dragons traded. One even bartered the shell jewelry that adorned many of their necks, forearms, and heads.

Dari saw a healthy and thriving community with sea dragon people who were not unlike those humans at home. These were not monsters, but thinking, rational beings who lived under the sea. The domes, as he had suspected, had been built for protection, but not to keep the water out.

Then the image changed as she showed an overhead view of the dome, which clearly showed the half-dozen of these circular communities within in it, each with housing caves, playgrounds, and marketplaces where thousands of the sea dragons thrived and lived. She showed him they were the dominant species in the ocean, taking his view along as several of them left to hunt the bigger creatures, such as the squidie and a colossal beast that rivaled an angular whale. She indicated that those animals threatened them.

But the different thing Dari noticed in the images was that the fish and the other sea life was not distorted as it now was. They looked normal, not like Picasso had created them. So, what had changed that? His stomach roiled as he began to have a terrible feeling about it.

As if to confirm his suspicions, his new companion showed him what he'd feared. Just beyond the dome, her mental projections showed an image of an object approaching the sea coming from the sky. Gigantic, almost the size of one-quarter of the dome, it darkened the water above the structure blocking the sunlight as it descended. Soon, it became apparent that the object would be coming down right on top of a section of the dome. The sea dragons frantically began vacating as quickly as possible.

The object hit the surface and dropped down into the water at least one hundred or more feet, bobbed up a little, then sank even lower. Huge swells of waves hit the surface of the dome and rolled through the openings into it. Sea life was disturbed, turning upside down. Eventually, the rolling settled and the object, a silver tube-shaped metal object stabilized and floated above the dome, still a couple of hundred feet from touching it.

As if she had been there, the sea dragon, whom Dari now called Alia in his mind, showed the search of one of her people who investigated the surface. His initial fears were confirmed. The object was a spaceship, likely the very one that had brought the settlers from Earth. A cargo door opened, and humans began sliding inflatable boats into the water and loading them up with a few of the crew and many more of the people who'd come to build a new life on Erinnua.

The boats set off toward the land and more were rolled out, the process continuing over the next few days. After the last people, the inflatables took many loads of supplies to the land. Dari's spirit ached with sadness for the sea dragon people whose lives had been disturbed by all this activity and the damage caused by the ship, but he still didn't see the destruction that had decimated the city.

But once the ship had been nearly emptied, something happened on board, and the crew began evacuating quickly, some jumping into the water and swimming toward the shore to get away from the ship. An explosion rocked through the sea, creating huge waves. Below the water, the vessel began plunging toward the dome, liquid fire streaming through the water as it crashed into the top, crushing the section he'd seen earlier.

Many of the sea dragons had returned to their homes and were killed when the ship crashed into it. Other sections sustained damage but didn't collapse. Almost all evacuated until the dome stabilized, then returned to begin removing and taking their dead to a place that looked like a giant cauldron where they vanished into a deeper section of the ocean. After that, they began repairs.

Dari saw the images as broken parts of the ship were hauled away on roughly-made sleds to a crevice in the ocean floor where they were dumped. But more than that, he saw two smashed power cells, like the ones that used a reactor to power the vehicle. This wasn't good, he thought at once. He didn't understand a lot about space travel, but he knew enough about reactors and the dangers associated with them.

Alia's images jumped ahead, showing him the rebuilt sections of the dome, although her people didn't attempt to repair the smashed section. But then he saw that the sea dragons had been affected by the leaked radiation from the ship, and they began to sicken. In a short time, they started dying. He now knew the terrible tragedy that had occurred here, and he wanted to weep for those lost creatures.

Feeling his sorrow, Alia projected a more recent image of the single inhabited circle that existed now with only a fraction of the sea dragons left. This was current, he realized. This was all that remained of her people. He dipped his horse head in reverence for her people. Tapping his shoulder to catch his attention, Alia raised her dragon hands with her clawed fingers spread to show him a number count, first ten folded fingers, then another ten and two more. Twenty-two. That was all that survived?

A sudden look of alarm crossed her features, and she gestured for him to swim away. He shook his head, not understanding what had upset her. She repeated the image of the squidie to emphasize the danger she perceived, then blew a stream of water from her snout, pushing Dari away, as if to warn him of danger. When he started to object again, he glimpsed movement several yards behind her from just beyond the curve of the dome.

Another sea dragon approached, much bigger and ferocious-looking. Dari didn't have to see it in detail to know it was a male. This one radiated anger and possibly fury that an alien creature had invaded his territory. Or maybe Alia was his mate, Dari surmised, and he considered the puca a threat. He hesitated a moment longer as Alia once again urged him to go.

What could the newcomer do? Not kill a puca, but he could certainly do damage to his corporeal form. Not being the kind to actually enjoy being torn apart, Dari decided retreat would be the best course for his suddenly frightened pony half. Spinning in the water, he swam as fast as he could from Alia's sight. Somewhat aware that the big dragon would pursue him, Dari sought only enough distance to discretely transform to his energy form. In a flash, he shifted to the ball of energy and propelled to the surface with speed nothing in the water could match.

Rising above the sea, Dari spun around in a slow turn, noting the various land locations that were at least a mile in the distance, some much farther. He marked the position and darted toward the safety of the land.

Arriving back at the hillside plot of land he now called home, Dari settled into the damp dirt and relaxed while he thought about everything that had occurred. He looked forward to discussing it with Sheilan when she came back from wherever she wandered at the moment.

CHAPTER 6

Underwater Danger

"So, Dari, you're telling me that these people who came to settle the planet effectively ruined the sea in this area with the explosion of their ship?" Sheilan asked, her eyes going wide.

"Exactly. That is precisely what I have been trying to tell you. The seas are tainted because of the fuel they used. 'Twas that unsafe reactor-type fuel that caused the damage and nearly wiped out the population of the sea dragons. Very few of them survived, and it had an impact on all the sea life in the area. That's why the humans have not gone back to the sea in all these years. Fear of the contamination has kept them away."

Today, Dari and the bean sidhe explored the area to the south of the O'Ceagan farm. While he admitted that the settlers had kept many things about Ireland on the new world, such as the speech patterns, the town names, and use of Irish words, they didn't actually speak the old language here anymore than they did in the homeland through the past few hundred years.

They'd just finished having afternoon tea at a shop with the same quaint look as any of the others on the planet. Dari mentioned it to Sheilan saying that it looked like they all came from the same template.

"Perhaps they have," Sheilan had agreed. "They might have had only one design on the ship, and the settlers held to it. They are still infants on this planet, Dari. In time, they will develop more individuality."

As they'd left and strolled into a park area with flowers and carefully cultivated trees surrounding a children's playground, the puca had told her about everything that happened and what Alia had shown him.

"The thing is," she stated, "all this knowledge has come from images you received telepathically from this sea dragon you have managed to connect with. Are you sure it is what happened or is it what she believes happened? Was she alive when the events occurred?"

She paused to watch a few of the children running on the playground kicking a ball around the field. This game also came with the spacers. These sporting contests were big events, he'd heard from the folks around the countryside. He mulled over Sheilan's question as one of the girls kicked the ball into the net, and it shot right past the defending guard. Sheilan had a point. He had not seen any of it with his own eyes, so it could be a passed on memory from Alia's people or a perceived recreation of the event.

"Well, you have me there, for sure. I cannot say that 'tis all true."

"There you go then. How can I take this to Grania without any proof to back it up?" She laid a hand on Dari's arm, meeting his eyes with a serious expression. "Listen to me, Dari. Next, there would be the question of whether we are interfering in human affairs or not. 'Tis not any of our business if they make a mess of their worlds or kill thousands of native animals or plants. While it may grieve us to see it happen, taking any action is not part of our function."

"I have no such restrictions," Dari objected, his eyes blazing. No sidhe laws told him what to do or not do. Pucas were independent creatures, subject to their own whims. If his whim wanted to do something to make the situation threatening the sea right, then it was his business.

"Do you not?" she asked. "I am constrained, lad. I have pushed it more than I should have in just coming here."

"Is there trouble?" he asked, knowing that she had not consulted with the sidhe council in pursuing her Earth family to the stars. But as she said, if a Banshee's function was to warn those of the bloodline of her family of impending death, what purpose would she have if there were none left to warn?

"Not yet, but I feel that it will surely be coming."

"Can the council even contact you this far from Eterien?" Dari had little knowledge of how the universe worked and struggled to even understand that there were different levels of it. Sheilan described them as dimensions or levels that existed side by side in the same space. His mind boggled to grasp it and failed for the most part. But he understood enough to know that it could be distant or close to where they were.

"I believe they can use the soil to extend their awareness of where I am and send a telepathic message. Can any come through the soil to us? That, I can't answer, but I suppose that it is a possibility. If we can use it, then someone from the council probably could as well." She rubbed at her shoulder as if she felt a sudden chill.

She looked away and into the distance, her eyes searching for something that neither of them could see. At times like this, she could make even the puca a bit nervous. Then she shook herself and turned to him again. "If it is my advice you want, Dari, then I would say to stay clear of the issues or problems of this world. They are not our fight, so to speak, and the races who live here need to work them out for themselves."

"Can we not help them along? The ocean people cannot communicate with the humans, who are probably not even aware other sentient beings are there, or that their Earth technology has killed and reshaped the undersea world." For some reason, passion surged through his often wishy-washy spirit at the injustice of this situation. Especially if the humans might have a way to repair the damage or at least stop the advancement of it.

"You risk exposing what you are to the humans as well as to the others. Although it appears you may have already done that with the sea dragon. She has seen you change, has she not?"

Dari dipped his head, admitting that he had indeed transformed in front of Alia. But he had done it numerous times over the centuries, just not in front of anyone who could label the change as anything more than a hallucination or the result of too much drink.

Sheilan turned and began walking back the way they had come, returning to the village and their hill beyond it. When they entered the edge of a forested area, she vanished, changing to her energy self in an instant and without warning. Not expecting it, Dari jumped with a start, but he soon followed suit. Clearly, she considered it the end of the conversation.

Instead of traveling to the hill, Dari zipped to the seashore where he could sit and meditate on the situation and what he must discover in order to convince both Sheilan and Grania that something needed to be done. The concerns of a puca failed to carry much weight with either of them.

* * * * *

Over the next two days, Dari returned more often to the seashore, his thoughts raging about Alia and her people as well as the misshapen fish he'd encountered. Images of the spaceship crashing, and the eerily-glowing power units leaking radiation into the sea continued to haunt him. Sleep for a sidhe is not actually that, but a recharge period while the mind continues to review everything that might be pertinent to its function. Usually, he concocted ways to pull jokes on humans or wreak a little havoc in a village. That was his nature, so he found it quite unusual to have something like this continue to revisit his thoughts.

On the third day, he transformed into his water horse form again and returned to the sea. This time, he looked at it through his admittedly distorted horse eyes with a new perspective.

What might these oddly twisted denizens of the sea have looked like prior to the accident caused by the landing? Were the strange shapes of the plants and shell creatures the result of leaked radiation over time? Had they, at one time, looked more like the sea life on Earth? Why did Alia's race not seem to have changed as much as the other creatures in the water? Was there some protection in the domes and caves of their city? Had they always had a crystalline look or was that also a result of the accident?

Dari wondered how far the damage extended. He knew it managed to affect the lakes, ponds, and streams on the land and that no water was consumed by humans without first being treated in purification plants. But the animals drank it, so were they affected by it as well? Perhaps six legs had not been the norm on the planet before the ship arrived. Had the new immigrants covered up the details of that disaster from the future generations by not revealing it and merely passing laws to prevent people from going into the water?

While Erinnua was a small planet, about one-third the size of Earth as Sheilan has explained, a good portion of it was water.

Had the devastating contamination spread to encompass all of it?

Somehow, he had to get the information he would need to convince anyone to do anything about it. If it meant telling the authorities that he was a sidhe, which they probably didn't believe in anyway, then so be it. In some matters, he simply could not stand back without trying to make a difference.

Or maybe his weak puca mind really was besotted by Alia as Sheilan suggested.

One of the talents, if you will, that pucas and several other sidhe possess is the ability to transform into another shape with most of the properties of the life form they choose to emulate.

Dari didn't exactly understand how this process worked, but he knew that if he could get a sample of the body's tissue, then he could duplicate the form although the personality within the construct remained his own. As Sheilan explained it, they were able to pull pieces of the things around them, what humans called molecules, to build the forms based on some kind of code that was written in the tissue sample. For the most part, he never concerned himself about how it happened just accepting that he could do it.

One of the positive things about building a form this way was that it made communicating with others of that body type easier as so much of the basics of their language was transmitted through the pattern that came from the tissue. So, all he needed to do would be to get a sample of a sea dragon's flesh or even one of those scales. He felt a surge of excitement at the prospect of trying out that powerful-looking form.

With this in mind, Dari returned to the sea, using his energy form to get back to the dome city where he changed into the water horse once he plunged into the sea. Then he called out to Alia, hoping she would answer. At first, he had no response, but he continued to swim closer to the dome, circling in the opposite direction from the way he'd come before. He repeated the call to the sea dragon, sending those familiar images of friendship that they had established, over and over again along with encouraging emotions.

At last, a tentative answer came to him. Dari sensed her fear and uncertainty. Once more he sent reassurances, along with, he hoped, a sense of urgency that he needed to see her. She showed an image of her pulling back away from Dari and of the big male sea dragon's anger. Frustrated, Dari tried to reinforce the image of friendship and the need to meet.

For a while, he got nothing, then she signaled that she swam toward him, so he waited. In a matter of minutes, Dari saw her rounding the curve of the dome, her seal-like appendages working like paddles in the water to propel her forward quickly. He studied the movement, thinking what it would be like to have those flippers and use them in that way.

She approached to within a short distance from him, then she stopped and waited, rocking in the water like a seahorse. Now for the difficult part, he thought. He needed to let her know what he wanted to do, so he pictured her in front of him and showed his horse mouth taking a nibble from her arm, just a tiny bite.

Shock and outrage burst toward him in response. More negative reactions, a resounding no in any language. He tried to soothe her and assure her that he wasn't going to really harm her, that he only needed a sample, but Dari didn't have the images to make it clear to her.

Alia backed away, whirling around and putting more space between them. He swam after her, repeating his friendship images without much success. He was about to give up when the male sea dragon came shooting around the curve, his flipper paddles churning the water behind him.

Dari sensed the fury as he came toward him, bypassing Alia along the way without so much as a glance at her. Clearly, Dari was his target. In a split second, the puca realized he had both an opportunity and a dangerous situation. Sheilan had warned that it could be unsafe for him, but while the sea dragon could severely damage the construct Dari wore, he couldn't kill him.

Dari shifted his posture to attack, determined to show him what a water horse could do. To be frank, Dari didn't think he actually had a chance, but all he needed was to get one bite on him. If he moved fast enough, he could do that before the bigger creature did too much damage. He kicked backward with his tail, straightening the horse form out to a more linear shape and flipped his tail through the water shoving himself forward to meet the sea dragon.

At first surprised, the sea dragon altered his trajectory a little to try to meet Dari head on, but the puca proved wilier than expected as he dove beneath his attacker. Dari opened his mouth to bite into the flesh as the underbelly sailed just above him. Faith, if he'd expected a soft expanse of flesh, Dari was truly mistaken. The leathery skin turned out to be tough, worse even than a water lizard to bite through, but the puca did manage to rip off a piece of a shimmery scale about the size of a quarter which he swallowed at once. The sea dragon turned on him before he completed the pass, ravaging Dari's back with his clawed talons. His skin tore like multi-bladed knives had ripped into it. Pain ran through the puca as he flipped around to make an ascent. Like a real equine, the water horse form bled quite a lot. In the end, that might have made his escape from worse damage a little easier.

Startled by the red blood in the water, the sea dragon reared backward with his flippers reversing his direction. The color seemed to perplex him, and perhaps he'd never seen anything quite like it before. As Dari flipped his tail to propel upward, he made an effort to slap the sea dragon in the snout, then he swam as fast as he could away from the dome. The salty water burned the gashes in his back adding to the pain in the body he wore. The gouges were dreadful, but far from fatal. When he reached a safe distance away from the sea dragon, he would begin pulling molecules to repair the cuts and stop the bleeding.

Glancing back, Dari realized the sea dragon had turned to pursue him again. After a quick survey of his surrounds, he darted behind a massive pillar of something resembling coral almost running into a sea snake. With the creature as startled as the puca was, he seized the moment to switch forms to his energy one. He didn't dash for the surface, but floated up more slowly, watching as the sea dragon pursued him around the coral. The sea snake had been eyeing his golden form and Dari suspected it planned to try to swallow him, but as soon as the dragon came, the snake recoiled in surprise and retreated, diving for an opening in the coral.

The sea dragon circled the coral three times before he gave up. Dari would have chuckled if he could have. Relieved, he sent a bizarre image of a horse laughing to Alia. Then he sped to the surface and returned to the shore.

Feeling oddly spent of energy, Dari remained in his pure form rather than changing to a corporeal one. This lethargy sometimes happened when he had drained most of his strength. Perhaps he'd lost more than he'd believed in the injury to his water horse form. He slowly floated back to the patch of soil to recharge.

Chapter 7

Becoming a Sea Dragon

Dark had fallen before Dari emerged to the surface again, shocking himself that he had been so unaware of time passing. He had no recollection of the time spent in the soil before he'd felt energized enough to come out. Usually, he thought about things, so it appeared the drain had been sufficient enough that he experienced a kind of shut down. Curious, that was, so he made a reminder to ask Shielan about it when she next came by.

He floated up to one of the upper branches of the tree that overlooked the plot and settled in it, looking a bit like a will 'o the wisp back home, a glowing golden object floating suspended just above a cluster of leaves. In this form, he viewed things in fractal patterns rather than in the more solid forms that a human construct perceived, so the leaves appeared as curved lines and sparkling dots of lavender energy, which is how the life force radiated on this planet.

Even when he studied the landscapes–mountains, rocks, and other inanimate objects, they looked more like a three-dimensional diagram, what Sheilan once said was like an architect's rendering, whatever that was. Even then, they still glowed with energy lines as it seemed that all matter had this power pulling it together. It confused him to think about it, but the base reality was ingrained in his own base form.

Adding to that, even the little bit of scale that he'd managed to bite off the sea dragon had been converted into this primal force with the pattern inherent in the flesh. Dari was aware of it in the sense that he could begin to see the shape of the creature in his own essence. While he could not yet transform himself into a sea dragon, he knew it would be complete in a few more hours. Then he could draw on the molecules to form the construct.

He chuckled as he considered that this transformation would, no doubt, startle Alia as she would perceive Dari as a sea dragon who looked almost identical to the fiercely protective one that she'd witnessed in battle with the puca. He hoped that she could still detect his unique telepathic signal and know his real identity.

He allowed his thoughts to drift back to his homeland, not Ireland, but Eteria where other pucas might be visiting or living these days. Never a large number of his kind, perhaps only a hundred, many had returned to their home when the humans grew more communal and began living and working in cities after centuries. In short, people pretty much quit believing in pucas and seldom wandered alone into areas where they might encounter them.

Perhaps he should have gone with them, but what was the fun in that? His friendship with the bean sidhe had taken him to the stars and beyond and what other puca could say that? But their connection—his and Sheilan's—was through the soil they'd brought to Erinnua with them. If it had linked properly, he could go for a visit then return to this very spot. If not, well, he had no idea what that might mean. So neither of them had been in a hurry to find out.

Chaka, Sheilan's new kitcoon pet, came ambling up before he observed the bright glow of her energy form approaching. He projected a telepathic greeting, and her ball of light drifted up toward him.

I was wondering where you had gotten to, she thought-replied. *I looked for you earlier.*

I took meself on a mission. I think I have what I need to communicate better with Alia and find the wrecked ship.

What have you done, Dari?

Even in the telepathic thought, she sounded concerned. Oft times he thought that she believed him incapable of taking care of himself as if he had no more sense than a wayward child.

Nothing serious, Dari answered. *But I did get a pattern sample of the male dragon.*

And—? She queried after a long pause.

And what? I got it, I survived although I do admit that I got a tiny bit beat up in the process, but I healed.

She drifted back to the ground and changed to her maiden construct. After so many centuries of doing it, she had no trouble changing her appearance and clothing, although the basic forms still remained the maiden, the mature, and the old female forms with simple hair, decoration, and clothing changes. Tonight, she wore a tunic dress that hit just above her knee, a fashion that seemed popular with the women in town.

"That was risky," she said aloud as she picked up Chaka and scratched his ears. The creature cuddled into her arms and chittered. "You do not know how the bodies of these native life forms might affect you or possibly harm you. Just because they resemble Earth-based life doesn't mean that you will be able to access them the same."

He flew down beside her and changed to his young lad form. Not as adept at conjuring clothing, he often arrived either naked or half-clothed as he did now. He sat next to the tree and thrust his bare legs out, crossing them at the ankles.

"I have almost completed processing the pattern, Sheilan. I do not think there is anything to worry about. As near as I can tell, it does not look significantly different from any of the other ones I have stored. 'Tis still made up of molecules and cells that may have a slightly different structure when formed."

"'Tis still not a wise thing to do. Do you not have any britches to put on, lad?"

"Stashed away somewhere, I suppose. I think I put clothes under a rock around here."

She rolled her eyes.

"If you recall over three thousand years ago, we took a risk in duplicating human forms, did we not? There was no guarantee that would work either. Yet it worked out with no harm to our true form, and we still can do it." Dari allowed himself a moment of self-congratulation for coming up with that argument.

"Yes, that is true, I suppose. But if you recall, at our creation, our forms were programmed to handle Earth life forms, and mine was limited to only three female forms. You, on the other hand, could turn into a worm if you chose to do it, but you have sense enough, I presume, not to turn into something that could be easily destroyed by another creature." She lowered herself to the ground next to him and turned Chaka loose to wander around the woods.

"Well, I did not do that this time. The sea dragon looks to me to be the dominant sentient creature in the sea. In fact, it might very well be the main life form on this planet. Why are you so opposed to my helping them, Sheilan?"

"'Tis not that I am against it, but it is something that is beyond our function, puca. 'Tis even against your nature to care much about any other life than yourself, yet I suppose you have already countered that by befriending me and showing some concern for the humans I serve.

"The bigger fear, my friend, is that it will reveal your true nature to the people of this world. If we are stuck here, it could be a real problem for you. And if the sidhe council learns of your transgression, it could end badly for you. Possibly us, if I am judged an accomplice, and I already have enough black marks with them for my own actions."

"I suppose you are right about that, but when did that ever give us any worry? In reality, is this kind of behavior not expected of my kind?"

She barked out a laugh. "Maybe so. You are a bad influence on me, puca."

"I do me best," he snorted out, a smug look on his impish face.

Sheilan leaned her head back against the tree and gazed up at the sky. Dari followed her gaze, taking in the view above them. The true moon, three-quarters full shone almost directly above them. Trailed by a glowing object that some might call a false moon, it was actually a floating chunk of rock called Boru's Relic, a sizeable phallic-shaped rock considerably closer than the moon that orbited the planet. It circled Erinnua three times within a day, so it was visible twice during the night at this time of the year and once during the day. Like Earth, the seasons changed, and that pattern would reverse in about six of their months.

Fewer stars seemed to twinkle in the sky here, although some were hidden by the moon's light, but Grania had told them it was because this sector of space wasn't as densely populated as Earth's view of the Milky Way, something Dari accepted at face value since he didn't understand much of it anyway.

Two fine features of the night sky here, he conceded, were the greenish-blue ball glowing in the distance beyond the moon that was the first of Erinnua's sister planets, Cardyff. The other one, an even farther distance away and not as bright, appeared as another blue ball with spots of green, yellow, and brown was called Caledonia, the third habitable planet of this star system. As Grania had explained, all three worlds existed in what they called the "greenhouse zone", a rarity in the galaxy, he understood, and close enough to each other to be easily visible.

"Do you think we might be able to travel to the other planets? I might like to see them, too."

Sheilan's head swiveled toward him, her mouth open with surprise. "What? After so many millennia of never leaving Ireland, do you now fancy yourself a multi-world traveler, puca?"

Dari shifted his gaze to his bare feet that he shuffled one over the other as he sat. "Well, now that I've come this far, I might as well see the neighborhood, don't you think?"

Sheilan rolled her eyes, but a little grin broke through. "Perhaps, Dari. Perhaps. The ships go to them from the spaceport, and even the Mo Croidhe stops at them on their runs, I believe." Pausing, she took a deep breath, then redirected the conversation. "So, if you can change into this sea dragon, what will you do then?"

"Now, that is a very good question and here is what I plan." He then told her what he hoped to accomplish with Alia and finding the wrecked ship. He thought he could determine if the reactors were still dangerous and formulate a report for the ship's captain if she could get him an audience with her.

"With Grania?" Sheilan questioned.

"Aye. She's the highest authority I know on this planet, so who else might I tell?"

"Well, I am sure that quite a few sit above her. Since this is a human colony, they will have some kind of government. But I suppose she would be a good sounding board for all you have to say and advise you well. Now, be taking extra caution in the waters, Dari. I cannot help you there."

The puca dipped his head in acknowledgment, knowing that he was indeed on his own in these strange waters.

* * * * *

As the morning light broke, Dari sensed the completed pattern within his memory. He could now make the transformation to a denizen of this sea. Enthused, he shot out over the water and dropped into the darker waves, a ball of translucent light looking like a tasty treat to any passing fish or even a squidie thing if one could catch him. He had no intention of remaining in that form for long. He concentrated on the dragon form, tapping into his energy source, then reaching for the molecules he needed to create it. Soon, he felt the body beginning to coalesce into a solid construct.

Feeling an odd, unnatural sensation, Dari realized the body functioned differently, not at all like his water horse form as he had expected it to be. His mouth proved non-functional initially, and he lacked oxygen, almost choking before the gills formed and began working. Next, the snout protruded and lengthened into the narrowed, seahorse-like one featured prominently on the sea dragon's face that the creature used to exhale air blasts to propel other sea denizens away from him. When the flippers sprouted and formed, he tried to move them, the action feeling awkward. A sudden jerk in the wrong way and the ocean turned upside down until he realized what he'd done to himself with that awkward move.

What the heck was he to do with the ruddy tail that formed? He whipped it as he would a horse's tail and found that it more or less responded. Alas, the whack and abrupt pain of the stinging barbs alerted the puca that he needed more control and caution with this weapon infested appendage. He also discovered that it functioned as a rudder as well, assisting in quick turns.

After a few hours, more mishaps and upside down flips, Dari began to get the feel of the alien body. While the water still felt heavier or thicker than Earth's water, he learned the big sea dragon body moved easily in it. He suspected that the form he wore might be lighter in weight than his water horse. At least, he began to feel that he could control the body even if the swimming still seemed awkward and jerky.

Releasing the construct, his essence form floated lazily back to the shore where he transformed to his young lad figure and located the clothing he'd left there. As he pulled on a shirt, he reflected that it was likely a good thing that the humans didn't frequent the seashore often, or he just might upset a few of them with his naked appearance. The lad he'd based his form on had not only been handsome but also decently-endowed. Those young ladies from the town might well be shocked were they to see him without his clothes. Amused by the thought, Dari's chortle sounded like a horselaugh.

Still chuckling, he climbed the path back to the plot under their tree. Drained by the morning's activity, he leaned back against the trunk to reflect on his first efforts at the new form and to relax while he recharged his energy.

CHAPTER 8

Skirting Danger

By mid-afternoon, Dari deemed himself ready for the real test of his new form. He focused on the position in the sea for the dome and shot his energy self skimming across the top of the water to the location before he dropped below the surface and began forming the sea dragon again. Having done it once, the second time went much quicker, and he soon had the fully developed body completed and set a course toward the city.

Optimistic, he sent a telepathic message to Alia and discovered that his communication seemed not only stronger but clearer. Images he had not consciously created augmented the thoughts. Almost at once, he received a feeling of puzzlement from her. It seemed as if she recognized Dari's particular wavelength, but the content was not what she expected.

Who?

The question came back clearly to him, an alien language translated within his brain. He sent an image of his water horse being, followed by the sea dragon body, and thought his name. *Dari, new form. Do you understand?*

He felt the shock from Alia, the concept of the form change startling her. While he did not think that she fully grasped it, she began toward him to see what he was trying to tell her. Concern touched him, fear even, that he might be in danger here again.

I change forms, he tried to warn her, then she came from above him, circling down from the top of the dome.

Who? she repeated

Eager to clarify this, he sent her his name along with his water horse image again, showing it changing into the sea dragon.

Circling down, she flipped in front of Dari, about twenty feet from him, and her faceted eyes stared intently at the new sea dragon in her territory.

Gradifin? That be? Her message made it clear that her image matched that of the big sea dragon, who, he gathered, was named Gradifin.

I am Dari. I look like Gradifin. He hoped she understood what he tried to tell her.

She gawked, she swam slowly around him, and she came closer, little by little. *Not Gradifin,* she acknowledged, *but look like. How?*

I change shapes, he told her. *I am not your race, but pure energy race called sidhe.*

He could tell most of that meant nothing to her, but she was still studying his new body and comparing it to her companion or whatever he was.

Your name? Dari asked, wondering if he had interpreted that incomprehensible sound he'd heard several days earlier as anything close to her true name. *How do I call you?*

Alahigra. I be Alahigra. I be Raguran.

Raguran, he repeated, thinking that she was telling him her race. *You and Gradifin both Raguran?*

She nodded.

With an internal sigh of relief since the physical body couldn't do it, Dari felt he'd made great strides in establishing both understanding and a new connection with her. Now to get down to the business of what he wanted to know and if she would be willing to take him to the underwater gorge where the ship had been deposited.

He started by explaining that he wanted to help her and the rest of her people, but that he believed the ship presented an on-going danger to her. If Dari thought that he had trouble communicating that to Sheilan, it was nothing compared to trying to get across alien concepts to Alahigra, whom he still thought of as Alia.

He repeated things, presented the situation in different images, and tried to chop up her own telling of the story to show her what he meant. She had led him away from the dome area while they conversed so that Gradifin might not happen upon them, but Dari felt the unease within her through their connection. She still didn't understand what he was and why he'd come here.

The big breakthrough came about two hours later as, for the fourth time, he showed her the ship coming from the sky to land, then showed her the image of Grania's ship at the space station above her planet and impressed on her that this was above her world right now. If she could have gasped, he thought she might have as the reality connected, but Dari saw the shock in her eyes repeated numerous times through the faceted vision they both shared.

More danger? More falling cylinders?

He shook his head and tried to reassure her. *No. Ships are not on the planet and won't fall. People, humans–* He paused to show her an image of Grania, then of her brother Liam, and even Sheilan, though she wasn't human. *Humans live in ships and on land. They might fix problem. I want to help Ragurans.*

How? How you help?

Show me ship. Take me there.

Dari felt the negative response and the fear behind it. In all fairness, he could not say that he blamed her. If he were not what he was, he probably would have been as frightened. In some way, he felt that fear in the form he currently wore as well. The Ragurans had developed a deep, inherent abhorrence to the crevice where the ship rested.

She shook her head and backed away from him with a few paddles of her back flippers. *No good. Do not go there.*

I must. Dari showed her the image of the ship again, this time focusing on the glowing lights and stream of fluorescent blue that seemed to flow from it. *That is danger. I have to see if it remains.*

It kill so many. Almost whole colony. Only a few live. Away from colony when it happened. We come from them. Her mind voice sounded frantic as if she was living through it.

He persisted, as stubborn as a puca could be. *I must see. Show me to area. You stay away.*

She whirled in an agitated circle, a sea dragon chasing its tail literally. *No! You will die. It kill Ragurans. It kill all who come near. I no show.*

Okay. Calm. Be calm. Dari realized he was getting nowhere with this approach, but something else had occurred to him as she was frantically sending images to discourage him. While he saw them, he also viewed something else coming from the memories he appeared to have tapped into from Gradifin. Another perspective, another angle, and he began to suspect that he might be able to find the way from those images stored in his mind.

Be safe now, he told her and urged her back to the dome. Let her think he was going away, then he could test his theory.

He swam in the opposite direction, looking for a marker that he'd seen in his mind, something that would trigger another image for him. It took several minutes before he spotted the rock that looked like the top hooked into a loop, then he sensed that he needed to go to the left of it. He turned that way, swimming and looking for any other indicators that he should change his direction.

Come on, Gradifin. Show me something, he pleaded with the remnants of the other sea dragon's memories.

In response, he saw an image of the next underwater mark to look for and shifted his head around to scan for it. In some ways, he found it beneficial to see so many facets of the objects as he flicked his vision from side to side, and in other ways, it sometimes confused and distracted him. Getting more used to it, he, nonetheless, wished for just one image to focus on. A dozen or more impressions of the next follow-point sorted themselves out to match the image, and he followed it to the next, working his way farther and farther away from the dome.

While Dari felt he was making progress and the markers, if you could call them that, kept coming regularly to keep him going, it turned out to be quite a distance from Alia's home. He'd been swimming away from it for a very long time, and he could sense the sky growing darker above the water as sunlight gradually faded. He judged it must have been about three hours since he started swimming, and even though this body was powerful, he was beginning to feel fatigued.

He slowed as he felt an urge to eat seaweed or something, then he realized that the underwater growth had thinned considerably. Very little vegetation grew on the bottom, and only a few scrawny-looking reed-like things that might have been a colony of shell creatures clung to the dead-looking stalks. Signs he must be getting close. He was certain of it. As he'd gazed around, he noted that no other fish or beasties swam in this area of the sea.

Forbidden. The thought flashed into his mind. The Ragurans had somehow marked this zone off-limits to all sea life. This came from Gradifin, he was sure. Did he know where Dari was or even what he was? Could the sea dragon somehow follow him or tune into the thoughts he'd been experiencing? It made Dari nervous to think about it, but if Gradifin knew and chose to try to stop him, he'd have to come into the forbidden zone. Dari plunged on toward the deep crevice that he now knew lay a short distance ahead. A short way farther ahead, he spotted a bluish glow above the seafloor and could even make out the deep gash in the seabed.

Dari felt a little nauseous. 'Twas a new and peculiar feeling for the puca. In fact, it took him a bit to realize that the upset in the mid-section of the construct amounted to feeling ill. Never had he experienced that in any form he had inhabited. Involuntarily, he spat out a mouthful of some icky-looking goop through the snout on his face. Flying across the water, the expelled food dispersed some and sank to the floor. Disgusting. Dari changed directions to avoid swimming through it. That turned out to be the beginning.

He grew more weary and ill as he got closer, but he had to make it to the gorge. The last few yards proved a struggle, his body giving out little by little as he forced himself on. The crystalline scales on it started turning black, and some began to peel off leaving a raw sore behind. As the seawater burned against these tender places, Dari cringed with the pain, feeling like he would die before he reached his goal.

Buck up, he chastised himself. *You're an immortal, not this construct. You can't die.*

Maybe not, another voice in his mind that sounded like Sheilan said, *but the body you're using can.*

And that was the truth. His mind was so riddled with the pain and illness that he hadn't thought about it. He just needed to let the body go and return to his energy form. But he couldn't seem to concentrate on it, then he teetered at the edge of the gorge.

Mustering every ounce of strength he could, Dari peered over the edge and into the dark gully below where the once shiny shell of a spaceship jutted up like broken tubes in five pieces with the bottoms of them buried in the muddy bottom. In the split between two sections, Dari saw the bluish stream of radiation pouring from the reactor engines that still churned in the water, no doubt pulling water in for fuel and to continue running.

They still polluted the oceans and would continue to poison life around them. His weakened body dropped down on the side of the crevice and his head flopped over the edge as he tried to view everything and record it in his true memory. The engines looked like dozens to his faceted eyes, but his brain sorted it out. Then, as he thought that Alia had been right; it would kill him, Dari lost consciousness.

CHAPTER 9

A Curious Water Problem

Dari regained consciousness as he floated above the surface of the water, his energy ball pulsing in anxiety as the moon passed overhead. It was midway on its nightly journey, alone at the moment, so Boru's Relic had already overtaken its orbit, which meant it was around the middle of the night stretch. What had happened?

He was confused, uncertain where he was, then gradually, he began recalling everything that had happened. He had died under the water by the gorge, and he couldn't even tell if he was in the same place. But, of course, he actually hadn't died, just his dragon construct had perished by the trench.

Dari rose up a little higher over the water and assessed his energy as being quite low. But he needed to be certain of his location before he returned to the shore, wherever it was from his current position. He plunged back into the sea and went down deep enough that he could see the crevice, in a fractal form, a short distance away with the malevolent glow from it lighting the area around it.

Then the puca shot up into the air and rose about a hundred feet above the sea and noted that he could still detect the radiation beneath the water. If a ship flew over it, the pilots would probably see it also, so why hadn't anyone done anything about it?

He turned and got a reading on where he was, senses

searching for the fractal patterns of the mountains on the shore in the far distance and not detecting anything at first. Did he look in the right direction? Was he so far away that he couldn't see them? If he could have frowned in his energy form, he would have. He felt well and truly disoriented.

Follow my vibrations, Dari. Sheilan's mind voice sounded in his mind, and he took heart as he aligned his energy toward her.

Talk to me, ya beautiful bean sidhe, he replied and listened to her mental frequency as she scolded him about wandering off halfway across the sea without telling her that he was going. Let her rant. He was grateful to be able to focus on her unique signature to pinpoint the location as he followed it to the shore.

Sheilan waited on the shore for Dari, a small bag of Irish soil in her hand, and a cross look in her green eyes. She opened the bag as soon as he arrived, and he darted into it, dropping into the comforting feel of the moist dirt. With his energy at its lowest, he gladly let go of any conscious thought and shut out the world.

"We'll discuss this in depth tomorrow, puca," he heard Sheilan say. He got the vague impression she began climbing the hill, but that was the last he recalled that night.

When Dari took on his young lad form in the late hours of the morning, he still felt weary, and his body ached, a sensation he found quite peculiar. He puzzled over it as he considered that the construct was rebuilt each time he took on the form and nothing should linger from the previous time he'd used it. In short, it was not the same as the previous one. He stretched his arms and noticed bruising along them. How could that be? His back ached, and his knees wobbled as he took a few unsteady steps.

"Finally, you are up."

Sheilan's voice came from behind him, and he gingerly

turned around to face her. She looked beautiful, as always, unless she was doing something related to her function, like scaring the life out of one of her charges.

A frown cut across her perfect face. "You look terrible, puca. Your eyes are two different colors, they look bruised, and your hair is a dirty-looking dark red. I think you may have a problem with your pattern."

"Impossible," he declared and heard the squeaky rasp in his voice that shouldn't be there.

She raised an eyebrow in question.

"The pattern is in me mind. Let me be trying it again."

With annoyance, he released the construct and built a new one a minute or so later, or so it seemed. When he had formed completely, Sheilan was sitting on a boulder near the big tree, but he hadn't seen her move there.

"Ye gads, when did you sit there?"

"About three minutes ago. What took you so long?"

He shrugged, still feeling the weariness. "Would I be looking more normal now?"

She bit at her lower lip. "Um, no. Not at all." Then she barked out a sharp laugh before she got it under control.

"Tis not funny, Sheilan. Me pattern's been damaged. I cannot repair it without the original sample, and that lad's been dead for twenty-two centuries on Earth! What am I going to do?"

"Have you no other humans stored?"

"Only a harpist that I accidentally nipped in my horse form. He was trying to ride me. But I didn't like him that much, and this laddie was my favorite. I felt at home in his skin, so to speak." Dari flopped to the ground, dropped his head to his hands and pouted, his face twisting into a pitiful look. He had never felt so dejected before, and he'd never had such a thing as this happen to him.

"Dari, 'tis clear that the contamination from the ship's engines—the one you were so determined to find—had an effect on you whether you want to admit it or not. Perhaps it will heal as your energy form repairs itself, but it may not. I warned you that it could prove dangerous although I had no idea it might affect your true form."

"And what if it doesn't heal? What about me other forms?" Dari felt panic as he considered that his horse or his water horse--his prime construct— might not be the same.

"Maybe you should check them. I will let you know if they look off."

He nodded and stood, reaching out for the molecules to transform into the draft horse first. At first, it felt fine and natural, but there seemed to be something off in his pacing.

Sheilan shook her head slowly. "Hooves are off, one looks like it might be too small. Your eyes are yellow and not red-rimmed as they usually are and the mane is the wrong color."

What color is it? He enquired via their telepathic connection.

"Purple with strands of silvery highlights. It is quite pretty."

At this revelation, Dari grew fearful and changed back to his flawed lad form. He dreaded learning that his other forms were equally wrong. It wasn't that any of them were non-functional, to the best of his knowledge, but that the bedeviled ship's reactors had damaged his base pattern.

"Give yourself more time to heal," the bean sidhe advised. "Ah, Dari, we are in a strange world with no support from the sidhe. We need to be more cautious, my friend."

While Dari wanted to agree with her and say they could just be neutral, he challenged her instead. "Sheilan, who will help this world we have moved to if not us? The humans came a few centuries ago, and the ship they crashed into the ocean is still destroying the planet that you and I need as much as their descendants and all the indigenous life here need it. How can we stand by and do nothing?"

"What exactly do you think that we can do? A puca and bean sidhe? What in our composition lends itself to helping a physical world?"

Dari narrowed his eyes, setting his jaw in a stubborn line. "We know things is what. I have viewed what is happening to the sea, and it will eventually kill everything on the land as well. People here don't drink water unless it is purified, so they know something is wrong with the water. With the advances in their science, they should be able to fix the problem. But not if it stays hidden away in a dark hole under the sea that they either do not know about or pretend that it does not exist."

She turned to take in the mesmerizing view of the sea they enjoyed from their allotted spot on the hillside. A melancholy look touched her eyes, and her lips turned down. For a moment, Dari thought she might actually tear up.

Not the Wicklow Hills to the Irish Sea nor the Burren to the Atlantic Ocean, but still the same draw that the water had always held for humans and sidhe alike. How did these humans not feel the pull to the water and yet deny themselves the unity with it? Their ancestors came from a land surrounded by water where they fished, boated, swam, and made their livelihood.

The sea, lakes, streams, and ponds had been the first thing Dari had wanted to explore here. It was a prime element to his water horse, and he required that connection. Did they not know that a dead sea would mark the end of life for them eventually?

"All I ask, Sheilan, is that you contact Grania and ask her to talk to us. Let me present my findings and observations to her and tell her what I know of the sea life that is suffering from a human-caused problem."

"I will connect with her," the bean sidhe answered. "If she has her little bag of soil with her, I will go to her. Otherwise, I will need to send a message. I do not know if this will cause problems for us, puca. But I expect we will find out soon if the council is aware of what we do."

"Thanks be to you."

She dipped her head in a brief acknowledgment, turned from him, and started walking toward the O'Ceagan farmhouse. Dari released his form and drifted back into the soil to contemplate what he would say to the ship's captain and hoped he could convince her to take it to someone else.

Another full day passed, and Dari rose to the land feeling more whole although as soon as he changed to his laddie form, he knew that the pattern still remained flawed as he could see the fading bruises on his arms and legs. A new construct wouldn't have that if it wasn't picking it up from his base pattern.

As the light retreated from the sky, Glamour rose from the trees behind him, ready to begin her journey across the sky. The puca hadn't seen Sheilan or been aware of her being around during the time he had been recharging.

Dari changed back to energy and rose again to the top of the tree, then rested on a branch where he had a good view of the world. In his mind, the fractal patterns formed multilayered representations of the forms of everything on the planet. As he studied them, he began to see where there were breaks or weak spots in the pattern. It seemed to him they were stronger over the sea than the land and some extended for miles in the water. In general, the water was harder to see the breakdown unless he was in it, but these were clearly visible across the surface. Various colors showed in muddy-looking hues in the damaged zones, especially the red and the blue. He had not noticed this so much when he had risen above the sea to mark the location. Had his fractal sense been altered in some way to extend the analysis of the lines?

While Dari found it confusing, and he was not sure he was interpreting it correctly, he did think the lines and colors represented damage to the pattern of the sea and the life below. Whether he could explain this or even if Sheilan would agree with him was another matter altogether. If she were here now, he would ask her to look and tell her his thoughts on it.

After an hour or so, he switched to the young boy again, still sitting in the tree, and he dangled his legs toward the ground almost fifteen feet below him. He watched as Boru's Relic ambled across the sky in pursuit of Glamour, gradually closing the distance until they drew even, then the oblong rock moved in front and raced across the backdrop of the pale sphere to pass her before it continued on in its first orbit of the night.

T'was mesmerizing to watch and comprehend the actual science behind it. A younger race of people, who had never known the mechanics of the Universe, and a sidhe who didn't subscribe to it, would find the whole thing a work of magic and surely those were gods romping in the night sky.

"You are stark naked again, Dari. Do you never expect someone to come by and see you exposed so well?"

He glanced down at Sheilan, and his lips curved into a smirk. "It seems to me that clothing is unnatural and it constrains the body."

"That may be true, but these humans, they prefer to not be distracted by certain bits of the body. Therefore, they cover them up, and as long as you are going to show yourself in their presence publicly, you should comply with their convention."

"Aye. If one of them comes along, I will do that. Have you talked to Grania yet?"

She elevated herself, young woman construct and all, to sit on the tree branch beside him. "I have. I explained that we–and I said we to give it more importance, you understand–had discovered something that we felt was important, and possibly dangerous, to the humans and we would like to present the details to her. I did not elaborate or give her a clear indication of the subject thinking it best to keep her intrigued rather than come ready to deny the possibility. She said she would meet us at the seashore by Ogham Rock."

"Excellent," Dari replied, then added, "What is Ogham Rock?"

"You might not have noticed it. 'Tis a nine foot or so monolith up the beach a little from the cove where the humans have carved their Ogham symbols into it. I had to go look myself. 'Tis an easy landmark for her to find since I thought it best to meet at the seashore as we would be talking about it."

"Good thinking that. Would you be willing to do me a favor and change to your energy form and look over the water and tell me what you see?"

"Are you wanting me to look for something in particular?"

Dari shook his head. "I just want to hear your impressions of what you see."

She shrugged and in a second, she'd dropped the girl form and was a larger ball of golden energy on the tree beside him. Her power glow waxed and waned, floated up and down, and shimmied a little as she observed.

Without warning, she shot from the tree and out toward the

water where he lost track of her.

Sheilan? What is it? he projected.

No worries. I am just getting a closer look. Something is off out here.

Dari waited and did not hear more, so he tried to connect with her again but did not get a response. The time moved by, and it seemed a long time before he spotted her energy ball speeding toward the tree again. She slowed and alighted next to him, then switched forms.

"Well?" he asked when she didn't say anything.

"'Tis odd, for certain. The patterns are uneven and have breaks in them, places where it seems they should go through smoothly, and they either stop or wrap around another. Do you reckon that this an effect from the radiation?"

"I do. What about the colors? Did they seem off?" he asked.

"A little, but not that it was significant. Why?"

"They didn't look muddied or off to you?"

Sheilan shook her head.

"Well, then, I think I am seeing things a little differently also." Dari then explained what he saw when he studied the fractal constructs, the breaks, and the color variances.

"And you've never seen that before?" she asked.

He shook his head.

"Then, I think that may prove that the leaking radiation has the ability to affect even our kind. This is not good." She frowned at the thought and clucked her tongue. "What is to be done?"

The puca bit back the 'I told you as much' as it sat on the tip of his tongue.

They sat in silence for a little while longer, then Sheilan transformed and drifted into the plot of soil, presumably to recharge and think. At least, that was his plan when he changed and followed her into the ground.

Chapter 10

Seeking Help from a Friend

In the morning, Dari popped out of the ground to find Sheilan settled beneath the tree, playing with the kitcoon as she would a cat. The little creature batted at her teasing fingers with its tiny hands and tried to grab a berry that she held in them. Laughing, she gave in as the fingers locked around the fruit and tugged at it. She let the little fellow take it, watching as it stuffed into its mouth with a look of satisfaction.

As Dari took on his human form, she nodded to a pile of clothing, indicating he should put them on. Dari pulled on the breeches and shirt, then faced her as he swiped his hand through his reddish hair to push it back from his forehead.

"Are you hungry?" she asked. "I find my human form is craving some scones or an eggy cake of some kind."

"I could eat." Dari also found that when wearing a corporeal construct, he often craved food.

They set off to walk to the town on the other side of the woods, Dun Gallow, it was called, and it was large enough to have two food shops. Dari never questioned where Sheilan got money to pay for their food excursions, nor did he pry into her activities when she was not with him, just as she did not ask about anything he did not volunteer–present situation excepted. Although he did admit he wondered at times, a long friendship requires no explanations.

As they walked, she chatted about many things from the varying colors of the sky on Erinnua to the antics of her newfound pet. She even commented on the possibility of Grania involving the local government in the problem if they–specifically Dari–could convince her of the danger. She still fretted that he might have to reveal what he was, and by implication, she was to the local authorities. That was something that neither of them was keen to do.

When you are basically a ghost story or a fanciful tale to humans, revealing that you really exist and are part of a race of like beings can be dangerous and disrupting. While Dari was willing to take the risk– and really, what could they do to him? Lock him up? He'd just vanish– he didn't want to involve Sheilan in this.

But as she talked, he realized something below the surface troubled her that she wasn't saying. Finally, just as they reached the town, Dari asked her flat out. "Is there something on your mind that you just cannot put into words, Sheilan? It appears to me you've been dancing around it."

She stopped and gazed at the woods as if the answer might lie there, then peered along the path into the village for a moment before turning her eyes on the puca. "Ah, 'tis troubling business for me, Dari. I need to go back to Ireland, then from there to the council. They have been tugging at me, calling me to come. I cannot resist much longer, Dari. I am tied to them far more than you, and they will not stop summoning me."

"Do you think that it will be bad?" he asked, not sure what to say. The council consisted of the most powerful sidhe ever, and a bean sidhe is one of the lowest orders of the pantheon. He, himself, was non-existent on it as a chaotic sidhe had no standing.

"I do not think it will be good. I have overstepped my

function, and they may not be very understanding of my viewpoint. They never thought that the tribes we were assigned to would survive as long as they have, and they most assuredly did not expect them to leave Earth."

"So, you will need to try the soil transference?"

"I think I must. If it fails, then I either won't go and will need to take a ship back, or I will be lost somewhere along the way."

The puca felt uneasy at the prospect of being separated from her. She was the only one of their kind on this planet. "Wait until this issue with the ship is resolved, and I will return with you."

"Oh, Dari, you brave little puca. We do not even know if it will work, so why risk yourself for my transgression?"

"Because you are my dearest and truest friend."

Her eyes misted a little, and her smile looked a bit sad, then she smiled and tousled his hair. "Let us go eat before we do something foolish."

*****

As Dari waited with Sheilan for Captain Grania to arrive, he kept thinking about what he might say to impress the urgency of the situation on her. For all that he did have a sharp tongue and wit, he was not generally very good with making a clear statement about important things like this.

They stood a short ways from the Ogham Rock, which Dari had studied when they first arrived. The symbols on it didn't make sense to him, but then Ogham writing seldom did. Sheilan had chosen the seashore to meet since she felt they could talk freely without any other humans overhearing the conversation. Like him, she was touchy about who might learn of their existence on this world although he did make it clear there was a puca in the neighborhood. Thus far, Sheilan had not made an official appearance to any of the O'Ceagan family, so only Grania and her crew were aware of her true nature.

She'd brought her kitcoon with her and held it in her arms, stroking its head and neck. The creature seemed to like the attention as it wrapped its small fingers around her wrist and licked at her hand.

"I cannot say that Grania will be able to help with this, but she will hear what you have to say and can possibly find someone who can do something about it."

"You know, I am not good at talking about this kind of serious business. Telling a story, aye, that I can do with a flourish, but relating something truly important, that makes me nervous." He stared at his human-looking feet and wondered if he was meddling where he shouldn't be as Sheilan had suggested. What did a puca know of human matters? But this affected Alia and her people as well as the rest of the undersea life in this sector of the sea. Someone had to stand up for them.

Sheilan gazed out at the sea for a few moments, then turned toward him. "That may be true, puca, but you made a good case to me. You just do exactly that with Grania. And here she comes now."

Dari shifted his gaze to the hill where the tall, lithe figure of the auburn-haired captain of the Mo Croidhe approached them in her robust and purposeful stride. Uncertain though she may be of their reason for traveling to Erinnua, she at least knew what they were and considered them friends of a sort.

As she drew nearer, Grania raised a hand in greeting and called out, "Hello, there. I didn't expect to be seeing you two again so soon. How are you settling in, Sheilan?"

"Fine, fine, 'tis a grand place here, and I am enjoying

exploring it."

"Good. And you, Dari? You look different. Have you changed your appearance?"

"A little bit. 'Tis part of a bigger problem that I will explain." He had glimpsed Sheilan gesturing to him to not go into it yet.

Grania raised an eyebrow, then nodded and said, "Are you adjusting to our land well? A few days past, I heard rumors of a wild white beast in the woods frightening some young girls. Would that have been you?"

"I was just having a tiny bit of fun," Dari answered with a guilty tone in his voice. "They had no idea what a puca was so I thought a little demonstration was in order."

She gave her head a slow shake of dismay. "Dear me. What have I brought to my homeland? You won't be hurting any humans, will you?"

"Not unless they force me hand," he replied, giving her his honest word.

She clucked her tongue in disapproval, then addressed Sheilan. "And you've tamed a kitcoon, it appears. He's a darling little guy."

"That he is. I call him Chaka. Would you like to pet him?"

Tentatively, Grania stroked the animal's head, and it chittered in pleasure. "I tried to make a pet of one when I was about seven, but it didn't work out so well. You must have a way with them."

"Perhaps. But how go the repairs on your ship? Will it be ready to get underway again soon?"

With a deep sigh, she said, "It's going pretty slowly, I'm afraid. There are a lot of little things to be fixed, and it all takes time. I think it will be at least another twenty to thirty days. Liam has been keeping on top of the work, but he's fretting to get going again."

"And what news of your fellow, Vilnius?"

"He's still at Zabrowski Station and waiting for news on his transfer request. He thought it would come in sooner than this."

Dari recalled that Grania's boyfriend was assistant stationmaster on the space station near Earth and that he'd decided to put in for a job transfer to Tara Station that serviced Erinnua. Even though Dari, himself, had never had any romantic relationships, he could see where it would be advantageous to be closer together.

But all this chit chat was making him nervous, and he cleared his throat to get their attention.

"Yes, Dari, you have something to tell me. Sheilan says it's of concern to everyone." Grania turned her piercing eyes on him turning his insides to jelly. Now he had to deliver.

"Let me begin by saying that I consider this to be a serious situation, and it affects the seas, ponds, lakes, and other waterways...even the rain. In truth, I believe, it may eventually affect everyone who lives on Erinnua. To explain, let me tell you that one of my shapes is a water horse, and it is a favorite one, I might add. So, naturally enough, I changed into it and went for a swim in one of the lakes around here. Right off, I noticed that the underwater life forms are quite a bit different from the ones on Earth. So, I decided to go into the sea and look around. From doing that, I learned that the sea life is also different. It looks like it is distorted and twisted. Then I discovered a creature similar to my water horse, only it's a sea dragon, and I learned she was sentient. In fact, her people are quite intelligent and had a whole underwater civilization."

Dari paused as he noticed the line between Grania's eyebrows growing deeper.

"A sentient underwater race? And you say 'had' a

civilization. What happened to it?"

"Well, that is why I wanted to tell you about it." He took a deep breath and told her about Alahigra, whom he called Alia, and her people and what happened to them. Then he told her about his theories on the ship's engines, and the danger he felt they posed to not only the sea life but to the humans on the planet. "I have seen the broken ship and the live engines, Captain. They are spewing poison into the water. I believe it is what has affected my form, and the differences you see in me were caused by exposure to it for perhaps six or seven hours."

Grania was quiet when Dari finished, then she went to the hillside, folded her legs down onto the grass, and gazed out to the sea with a thoughtful expression on her face. He followed over and sat in the sand facing her. Sheilan remained where she was, waiting for Grania to comment.

"All my life I was told not to go into any water or drink the water of the planet. The only water we were to use had to be filtered through our cleansing plants. My brothers and I were told they were deadly or could make us very ill. We never questioned it. No one ever said anything about radiation or contamination from a crashed spaceship. The early designs of the ships were powered by fusion reactors, and they continued to produce energy so long as they had fuel.

"If what you saw underwater was a fusion reactor, then it is still burning fuel after almost two hundred years in the sea. You are quite right that it is a danger to the sea and to humans both. We take care, even when it rains, to avoid the water. For sure, the first settlers knew what the danger was, and yet, it seems they failed to record the information or pass it on for future generations to know."

"What can be done about it?" Dari asked, fearful that there

may not be a solution. He wanted so badly to help Alia and her people, as well as the rest of the ocean dwellers. As he'd said, he believed the problem concerned the whole world and hadn't Grania just confirmed it?

"Good question, puca," the captain answered, and she sounded almost like Sheilan when she said it. "I don't know. But I think this needs to be brought up with the governor of our colony to find out what, if anything, he knows about it, and if he has any ideas what can be done to fix it. We have many newer technologies now, so there is likely a way to neutralize it. I think I'll have a chat with Liam about it. He's one of the best engineers in the galaxy, so if anyone knows what might work, I would bet on Liam."

She flipped on a recorder on her jumpsuit's shoulder, then spoke again. "In order to present this the best I can, I need to ask you some questions about what you saw and the 'fractal view,' I believe you called it, and how it looked to you. Once I discuss this with Liam, he might be able to put it in better terms to explain to the governor."

Reassured, Dari thanked her for taking on the task, then answered each of her questions as honestly and thoroughly as he could. As they finished, he thanked her again for helping.

"Don't thank me yet, Dari," she replied. "I'll take the first steps, but I may need you to tell your story to the governor in person. Now, don't fret about it until we know more."

She added the last as she saw the alarm that crossed his face. Tell others what he knew? He couldn't explain without revealing his true nature, and even though he had considered this, facing the probability of it alarmed him.

Sheilan saw this and said, "As Grania said, don't fret. There will be time to work out a plan if it comes to that."

Grania climbed to her feet, unfolding as gracefully as she'd sat. "Thank you, Dari. It saddens me that humanity's landing on this planet caused such a disaster for Alia and all of the sea life. We didn't even know they were there. I'll be getting back in touch when I have some news."

With that, Grania spun around and headed back toward the village. Dari turned to Sheilan. "Well, that went well enough, I would say."

The bean sidhe nodded, but her expression told him nothing.

CHAPTER 11

Facing Off Against Gradifin

For the next two days, Dari waited for any word from Grania and tried to figure out what he would say if he had to speak to the governor. Telling the actual story of what he saw wasn't the problem. It was revealing how he had seen it. What would the official think if Dari told him he could change shapes?

He'd probably think Dari had taken a few too many pulls on the whiskey barrel and imagined the whole thing. But if the puca demonstrated to him that he could change shapes, then the governor might lock him away as a space alien, which he supposed that, in reality, he was and dismiss his ravings as a plot against the planet. 'T'was a dilemma, he admitted. He thought until his brain hurt, but he couldn't figure a way to actually tell the truth without lying about how he knew.

Finally, Dari took Sheilan's advice and set the problem aside until it became more imminent. He amused himself by playing a few tricks on the people of the two nearest villages. He soon learned that just the neighing sound of a horse could have a scary effect on people who had never seen one of the creatures. All he had to do was hide his pony-self in the woods and make the noise as a human walked by to make them jump in surprise and scurry away down the road as fast they could. No one was harmed by the joke except one round little man who was so startled that he bolted, tripped over a tree root in the path, and fell face first into the dirt. He had a few scrapes, but he still jumped to his feet and ran away without Dari even having to make a second sound. Although he did manage a horselaugh or two.

When he got bored of that, he went to the seashore in his human form, which was still not quite right, and he despaired that it would ever be right again. And here he sat, staring out at the water with a longing to go in it and sadness for what he knew was there. He tried a couple of times to contact Alia, but she either couldn't hear him or wouldn't reply. As he tried a third time, after waiting for at least twenty mites, Dari felt a telepathic touch to his mind, and he focused on it, expecting Alia's mind touch in return.

Instead, he sat back, shocked when he felt an angry, roaring dragon voice instead. Within a blink or two, he quickly discerned it was Gradifin. Where he shared a good rapport with Alia, and they could communicate their thoughts better, the big male dragon was harder to follow, the images seeming random. At first, Dari thought he was telling him to stay away from Alia, which he may have assumed was Gradifin's mate and the sea dragon thought Dari was infringing on his territory, but then Dari realized Gradifin was calling him out, telling him to come into the water and face him.

His better sense told Dari it wasn't a wise thing to do, but another part of him felt the challenge had to be met if he was to ever be able to deal with the Ragurans on this world. He stripped off his clothes and dashed into the water, swimming out to the deeper zone as quickly as possible before he changed to his sea dragon form.

With dismay, he realized at once that this particular form was still a little worse for wear. While it had formed mostly correctly, it bore bare patches on the skin where the scales had been erased from the pattern. Although his front legs seemed fine, he was short a talon on his right hand and the slightly irregular path of his swimming warned Dari that one of the tail flippers was likely a little smaller than the other.

No time to think about that now though as he spied Gradifin swimming toward him at a fast clip. Once in this form, the other dragon's thoughts became more explicit, and Dari clearly got the message he broadcast now.

Not take my form. My alone. You not Gradifin. You not Raguran. You not belong here. You stay away from Alahigra. Not for you.

When he'd finished that burst, Dari tried to reply telling him he was a friend and trying to help them. He could get help to end danger to them.

Help from above world? Not want. Gradifin's anger came through clearly. Maybe Dari couldn't blame him for not trusting any of the humans, but the big sea dragon could at least listen to what he had to say.

Broken ship still danger. Needs to be turned off and buried. Dari tried to show him an image of the ship's engines still active and what the area around the trench looked like.

It only angered Gradifin more. Whirling around in a fierce circle, he unwrapped his body into a charge at Dari. Caught off guard, the puca went on the defensive and ducked below him, diving toward the bottom. Gradifin shot past, but then came back around in an instant, plunging toward him. How in all the blessed lights in Eteria did he fight against this big fellow? The dragon form was barely comfortable on him, and he had no idea what technique to use. He hesitated until the sea dragon was nearly on him, then thrust his flippers upward, his long barbed tail whipping around as he rose to catch Gradifin in the shoulder. The bigger dragon exhaled a jet of water as it hit him, and it barely missed Dari's flippers, but managed to whirl him around again as

Gradifin swung toward him.

Dari brought his front legs up, as he would in his horse form where he would have hooves to kick out, but now he bore talons that he raked toward Gradifin. He responded in kind and Dari jerked as a swipe of his talon-tipped right hand cut across his chest, slicing through the scales and drawing first blood. Dari sucked water and gagged. Choking, he coughed, sort of, and spat it out. He'd discovered the snout wasn't designed for intake, only exhale.

While he was doing that, Gradifin came at him with his barbed tailing spinning like a bolo, which he whacked into Dari's mid-section. Sharp points of pain exploded as the spikes tore into the puca's flesh. A pure horse reaction, he spun around and kicked with the flippers, imagining them hind legs and the movement a sharp horse kick. Although not as effective as it would be on land, the broad tail flipped caught Gradifin in the side and knocked him several feet toward the shore.

By now, Dari had deduced that he was ill-equipped to tussle with the big sea dragon and resorted to a speedy retreat. Namely, he shifted to his energy ball before Gradifin could attack again. Dari sensed the sharp exclamation as the other saw his opponent disappear right in front of him while a golden light darted for the surface.

Dropping onto the sand, Dari quivered in his snug little ball and gave thanks for the instant change capability. Even now, he still felt the sting from the barbs and the ache of the bruising. Though he couldn't make out what Gradifin yelled at him, Dari knew he was agitated beyond words.

*****

"It sounds like you took a big risk there, Dari, and you're lucky that the big dragon did not do worse damage to you." Sheilan munched on a bunch of something that looked like pink grapes as she leaned back against the tree.

Dari paced back and forth as he related his story to her. "Not so much luck as being able to get away from Gradifin easily. But it has given me cause to wonder if fixing the problem is the right thing to do if you get my meaning."

"I am not sure that I do. You want to save the sea life by taking care of the ship problem, but at a word of resistance from one of the sea dragons, you are questioning if it is proper. Is that what you mean?" She popped another grape into her mouth and handed one to Chaka.

The creature accepted it with a gleeful chitter and took a bite as it held in it in between his paws. It was a cute little thing, and Dari admitted the kitcoon was growing on him.

"Not exactly that, no," Dari replied getting back to his dilemma. "I just question if involving the humans is the right thing to do. See, the concern is that they created the problem in the first place, so the objection Gradifin has is that he doesn't want any of the land people to fiddle around in their domain again. He is understandably concerned they might make matters worse. And he may be right. Can they actually fix the problem?"

Sheilan shrugged her shoulders and offered a little sprig of the grapes to Dari to try. "That would be a question for Grania and Liam, my friend. If they believe that they can do it, I have a lot of faith in them. But if they are unsure, then maybe you should worry and bring up the concerns that the Ragurans have. I had word this morning that Grania will be coming by tomorrow to see us and let us know if she has been able to arrange anything."

Dari studied the odd-colored fruit and sighed. "Strange that the food here is similar to home but not exactly like it. I miss turnips. Did the colonists not bring any with them?"

At Sheilan's shrug, he tentatively, pulled of a grape and popped it into his mouth, pleasantly surprised by burst of sweetness. Finding it similar to one of the tasty green grapes back home, he deemed it passably good.

He dropped to the ground next to her and said, "Well, then, I guess I will learn what the captain has to say and decide if we need to discuss the matter further. The thing is, I would like to do this with the Ragurans approval and support. I would not want them to feel that we are invading them again or acting against their well-being. But I am not sure I can convince them."

"There is always a way, Dari. Maybe the path lies through Alia. If there are other sea dragons, do they not have a voice in the decision? Maybe she can help you speak to more of them where you can explain what the danger is and how it can be rectified." Sheilan rose to her feet and stretched, her luminous eyes taking in the details of the area around them.

They hardly ever saw anyone in this field, not even the O'Ceagan family. Most times they left the shidhe completely alone, and the neighbors rarely came down the nearby road. The farmhouse sat a good distance from them, and they farmed the lower fields, but not the area where they had their small space. Perhaps it just wasn't needed yet. The population of the planet had not grown so much since the ship landing, so they thought it may be planned for future growth.

Dari recalled a time in early Ireland when it was similar to this, people living in small villages many miles apart and very few in the countryside between. Farmers had small plots, enough to support their families and to trade in the town for additional supplies. It was a simple life, and it worked well for many years.

Like Ireland, he expected that this would one day explode with growth and industry if that cursed ship in the sea didn't kill all the life on the planet.

"I am heading into the town," Sheilan said. "I have a few errands to run. You figure out what you want to say tomorrow, puca. You asked for the meeting, so if Grania has arranged it, you better have a convincing presentation." As she turned and started toward the path, the kitcoon scurried to catch up with her.

The conversation hadn't helped him to decide his next step, so Dari went back to pacing and thinking about it. Sheilan may be right; the answer may lie with Alia and the rest of the sea dragons, but how could he get the message to them without going up against Gradifin? Dari had a nagging feeling that he was the leader of the colony now, and he would still be the one that the puca needed to convince.

CHAPTER 12

Putting the Pieces Together

Dari dressed in his best garments to meet Grania at the Relic Pub in Dun Gallow. Not that they were much different from the ones he usually wore. He only had three total changes of clothes now that he'd lost one set. Sheilan had procured the ones he wore now, a pair of synslim breeches and a tabbed shirt that seemed to be popular with the folks in the village. Again, Dari never asked how she came by these things although he had his suspicions.

It did surprise him that the captain wanted to meet in a public house, but when he got there, Dari soon learned that she'd taken a private room upstairs where they could talk unobserved. He'd not been farther than the bar area of the pub, so he found it interesting that there were rooms to let above the main floor, much as there used to be in many places on Earth. Not that he'd ever stayed in one, but he knew about them.

The room they entered was quite nice, brighter than Dari had expected it to be with light colored walls and thin curtains that allowed the sunlight into the room. A bed pressed against a wall, but the area closest to the window had a table set up with four chairs and on it, sat a pot of tea with four cups, as well.

"Are we expecting another person?" Dari asked as he took the seat across from Grania.

"Liam had planned to come with me, but something came up on the station with the engines, and he decided he needed to stay to work with the repair crew. Would you like tea?"

"Indeed, I would," the puca replied. He was never one to turn down food or drink when he wore his human form.

Sheilan slid into the chair facing the window and said, "That would be lovely. Thank you." So formal. Then she asked, "I take it, then, that things aren't going as smoothly as you'd like on the ship."

Grania flicked her head sharply as she poured, then slid a cup toward Dari. "No, not that smooth. The delays in getting things fixed are troubling me, and it seems like each day brings a new problem. Little things, mostly, and I'm beginning to wonder if Grand-da ever actually repaired anything on the ship or just cobbled it together to make it work. Liam is fit to be tied."

"But he is the expert, you say. He knows what he's doing."

"Aye, that he does," the captain answered and slid over a plate with three different kinds of cookies on it. Dari took one with a red jam in the middle and took a bite. Quite tasty and just a bit tart. He decided he wouldn't mind eating a few of those.

"It's why he prefers to stay on the ship while they're working on it. He knows the ship well and what to look for," Grania continued, then she cast a knowing eye at him. "And he knows quite a lot about engines, mind you. That's why he wanted to come today. He wanted to talk to you about the reactor you saw, what it looked like, and how big it was. I don't suppose you have any drawing skills, do you?"

"You mean applying a pencil to paper?" Dari asked in astonishment. "Why, no. I never tried it. But if you hand me some, I can give it a go."

"I may have a better option, Dari." She pulled out her computer tablet and keyed something in, then touched the screen in a couple of places and turned it toward him. "There. I have called up images of four of the reactors that were used in ships at the time. Do any of these look like the one you saw?"

Dari took the tablet in his hands, marveling at this gadget that she used. He'd seen them, of course, but never before held one in his hands. It showed the images as clearly as if they were right before his eyes. They all looked similar with only slight differences, one of them being size and another being shape. The one he'd seen was more of an egg-shape than a ball shape, and only one of the ones Grania showed him had that look. He pointed to it. "That one."

She turned the tablet toward her, tapped on the image and another page came up showing more pictures of it, but again with slight differences. Dari frowned as he looked at them, picturing the scene at the gorge in his mind. He had seen the glowing object through the dragon eyes, and it made it more difficult to focus in on the differences, but then he recalled a detail that he'd barely noticed at the time. The engine had a mark on it like a pitchfork, just the head part. He peered at the images and shook his head, then he told Grania, "The one I saw had a triple pointed symbol, like a forkhead at the top of it."

Grania thought a moment, tapped the screen again, then opened a single image to show him. There it was – the same image.

"It's a Trident Corporation logo," she told them. "They put it on their engines and reactors to identify them. If that's the one you saw, Dari, it will help Liam to figure out how to shut it down. He wants to go out with a friend of his and you to take a look at the area and see exactly what the situation is. Will you do that?"

"In a ship?"

"On a shuttlecraft flying to it where it can hover over the area and collect data," she clarified.

"Not a sailing vessel then?" he asked.

"No, not this time. Maybe when they go to shut it down. But to gather information, if the governor approves it, they'll take the shuttle. Will you go?"

"Of course, I will. Anything I can do to help."

"Excellent. Now for the real news that I have. The governor has agreed to see you, and it will be three days from now in Abḥainn Mhór at thirteen hours, just after lunch. So, I will come here, to this very tavern, with a ground shuttle at ten hours to fetch you and take you to the meeting. I'll bring along a suitable change of clothing for you, so you look a bit more presentable to meet His Honor."

He straightened up, looked indignant. "These are me best clothes. Are they not good enough?"

"They're very nice clothes, Dari, but you would make a better impression with a little upgrade to them. Like pants without a rip in the pocket and a shirt that might fit you a little better and a light jacket over the top."

Grania's green eyes and pleading expression begged Dari to consider it. Then Sheilan threw in her own opinion.

"Listen to her, Dari. She is trying to help you to impress your reliability upon the governor."

Grania tipped her head toward Sheilan and raised her eyebrows in question as if to ask if he would take her advice.

"Very well," the puca conceded. A new set of clothes wouldn't be bad, he decided, and if the captain kindly brought them, it would not be neighborly to refuse. Turning his attention back to the bean sidhe, he asked, "Are you coming with me, Sheilan?"

She looked a bit uneasy, then said, "I do not know that my presence would add any weight to your presentation, and it may be better if I stay completely out of it. You are the one who needs to tell it. You will have Grania and Liam there on your side, so you have the best support you need to do this."

Dari's shoulders drooped a little as he thought about facing this without her. What she said was true in that all she knew about it was what he had told her. He supposed that if she went with him, she might risk revealing herself as a sidhe as much as he did.

"You're most certainly welcome to come with us," Grania said. "There's plenty of room in the transport."

Sheilan looked apologetic. "Thank you for the kind offer, but there are some matters I should attend to here. 'Tis best I stay behind this time."

Grania shot a worried look her way, no doubt thinking about the bean sidhe's official function. He wondered about it himself.

"No, 'tis nothing to be concerned about, Grania. All is well at this time. It is not related to your family in any way."

The captain sighed in relief, then passed another plate of cookies his way while she refilled his teacup. As Dari bit into a spiced cookie, he pocketed another in his pants and tried not to think about the ordeal ahead. A puca facing an official of the country? None of his companions back in Ireland or in Eterian would believe a word of it.

*****

When Grania arrived with the ground shuttle, Dari grew excited to see the modern, sleek-looking vehicle that floated above the ground, much like the ones back on Earth. With the way that the people lived in ancient-looking villages, he had half-expected some kind of smelly, oil-fed contraption that resembled a carriage.

Not only was the shuttle new, but it had a separate area with a facility that had enough room for him to change into the more suitable clothing that Grania had brought for him.

That turned out to be new dark blue breeches made of a stretchy-type fabric that fit quite comfortably on his slender body. Made of the same material, the shirt was a lighter blue and appeared to mold itself to his torso but felt a bit tight around the neck where it barely left room enough for him to breathe. The short coat to go with it was light tan with blue accents at the front opening and along the sleeve hems.

He gazed in the mirror to get a good look at himself. Shaggy reddish-brown hair that fell in his eyes, and tumbled down to his shoulders. Perhaps it should be cut.

His widely-set eyes were two different colors now, brown on the right side and grayish blue on the other, thanks to the pattern break. He ran a hand through his hair, pushing it back away from his eyes and wet it a bit to keep it slicked back. The face itself was pleasing with a straight, turned-up-a-tad-at-the-tip, nose. A few freckles dotted his cheeks on each side of the nose, and his full, nicely formed mouth hung slightly open. 'Twas a fine Irish face, and he still recalled the jovial lad he'd borrowed the form from so many centuries ago.

Grania also provided new footwear for him, shoes that slipped on easily and clung to his foot comfortably. Also dark blue. Dari admitted that he looked quite presentable.

Now if he could just manage to do as well with the recitation for His Honor. He'd practiced it several times in the past two days, and Sheilan had played the governor, asking potential questions he might have. He hoped that they had covered all the possibilities. The one that worried him was the one he was sure the governor would ask: How do you know this information?

And the truth of it was that he had seen it with his own, more or less, eyes, and he had been in the forbidden waters.

As Dari came back out and sat in the seat next to Grania, he asked, "Is this suitable, Captain?"

"Very suitable, Dari. You look very nice, except for…" Her voice trailed off, and she bit her lip as she looked at his hair.

"Might there be time for a barber?" he asked, relieving her of saying it.

She pulled out her tablet and tapped in a few words, then it changed pages again, and she added a little more. "Yes, 'tis all set. We'll take care of it as soon as we get to Abhainn Mhór."

"How long might that be?"

"We will be there in about thirty mites. Relax and enjoy the ride."

So, Dari did. He leaned back and gazed out the window at the passing countryside and watched as the villages turned into larger cities as they got nearer to their destination. He had missed all this on the trip in. Because of their lack of proper papers to travel, Sheilan and Dari had arrived on the planet, and at Grania's family home, in the travel trunk the bean sidhe had brought onto the spaceship. In their energy forms, they had stayed in the lower portion, secure in the Irish and Eterian soil within it.

"There's the city, just ahead. See that tall building in the middle of the skyline? That's where we're going."

She pointed to the only thing that stood well above anything else in the city. Compared to the buildings in Derry, Dublin, and Shannon, this building was little more than a toddler. Probably not more than six stories high. But for this planet, that was saying something, Dari presumed.

"Is it the tallest on the planet?" he asked.

"That it is," she replied and looked at his face. "You're not too impressed, are you?"

He gave her his are-you-joking-look.

"Well, I know. I've seen the big buildings in Tokyo and that monster in Dubai that grew even taller after it was rebuilt. I've also seen even bigger ones on other planets, but for Erinnua, this is quite remarkable. You've probably noticed that our towns and villages are mostly rural and built in imitation of old Ireland. That was by choice. The settlers who came here wanted to return to that simpler life and chose to make the homes and towns the friendly, small ones that their ancestors spoke of so fondly."

They zipped down an avenue broad enough for several vehicles to go abreast, then the shuttle pulled into a parking bay near the city center where that tall building of six stories and a bell tower loomed over the metropolis from across the avenue. As they got out, a tall, handsome lad came bounding toward us. Liam had been waiting. With him, a slightly shorter, blond fellow with long hair pulled back into a knot at his neck greeted us, and Liam introduced us. This was his friend, Trigg Knowlson, a mate from his academy days, and a man who knew all about the engine reactor we wanted to shut down.

Dari felt entirely too short standing next to these towering men and decided, then and there, that he would need to get a bigger, stronger human pattern. Liam took charge of him then, leading him to a hair emporium, which he explained was what they called barber shops and women's salons on this planet. This did not reassure the puca, nor did the look inside that was entirely too frilly for a man to be in, but Liam said it was fine.

To make matters worse, the barber was a woman. But she smiled and seemed friendly enough, although that didn't mean she knew anything about cutting men's hair. She introduced herself as Angela then showed Dari a few images of possible haircuts with his face plastered on the image. He picked one he thought looked good, a little shaggy but not long. She agreed it suited him, then began trimming his hair with quick, deft snips of her scissors.

Within fifteen minutes, he'd been transformed. He looked like a new lad and quite cosmopolitan, Dari decided, thinking that was the word Sheilan had once used to indicate someone who looked city-like. When Liam saw him, he gave his approval by holding a thumb up. They met up with Grania and Trigg, who sat at an outdoor eatery in the patio of the government building.

"We ordered for us all. You look great, Dari." Grania's smile reflected her approval.

Dari grinned in appreciation and sat, but now that they were here, with that official-looking building crouched so near, he wasn't sure he could eat anything. The time had almost come to try to make his case, as Liam had put it on the way back from the shop.

Then the food arrived, presenting dishes too tempting to pass up even for a puca.

CHAPTER 13

Presenting His Case

As Dari passed through the big, heavy wooden door to the governor's office, his stomach did little flip flops, not something he would usually feel, but just being around this much authority made him nervous. Grania stayed by his side as Liam and Trigg went in first without a care in the world. They introduced themselves to the skinny little man who sat behind the desk and called him Governor, so that was who he must be, Dari concluded. Then Liam turned to introduce his sister and Dari, and he found himself pushed to the front and taking the hand the man held out to him.

The governor sported an admirable head full of gray hair and friendly-looking periwinkle blue eyes. He indicated that we should sit and said, "Well, then, Mister – uh, Dari, is it? It seems you have a story to tell me that you think is of importance to the entire planet. Is that right, lad?"

Lad? Dari questioned in his mind. Of course, to the governor, the puca looked like a youth and not an old spirit who had roamed the land his ancestors had come from, so he would give him that as a valid point. Speaking up, he stated, "Aye, sir, that I do. I'm not really very good with the words, so I will tell you this as simply as I can. You see, I like the water and going into it. I am not from Erinnua originally, you understand. So, I did not know that it was forbidden to go into the water here, and I went into the sea for a swim."

The governor blinked at Dari, a little surprised by this, he guessed.

"Well, what I found down there was quite strange. The sea life is twisted, distorted if you will. As I went farther along, I encountered an undersea race of sea creatures who are sentient. I believe that's the word. An animal that has the ability to think and be self-aware is how I understood it." Dari glanced at Liam for confirmation, and he nodded.

The governor dipped his head in agreement and said, "A sentient race under the water? How do you know this?"

"Ah, here is where it gets a bit tricky. I can communicate telepathically with other telepathic races." Dari said the words a little choppily, not sure how the governor would take them.

The man looked over the puca's head to raise an eyebrow at Grania. "He is fey," she said, and Dari shot a glance at her. Did she just tell the man he was one of sidhe? Wasn't that what these humans referred to with fey?

But the governor seemed to take it in stride. "I see. So, you are underwater and communicating with this sentient animal, is that right?"

Dari nodded.

"And what did you learn about this?"

He took a deep breath and plunged in. "The creature I contacted is a sea dragon. Her name is Alahigra, but I call Alia. Her people live in a dome on the sea's floor, and at one time, it was a thriving colony with thousands of them in it. Then the giant silver tube came and destroyed a section of the dome, killing many of them. But worse than that, as I have learned, the tube was actually a human spaceship that crashed into the sea."

Dari watched the governor's eyes widen as he related his

story. Next, his eyebrows lifted in surprise or shock. The puca couldn't tell which.

Nonetheless, he continued. "From what Alia related to me in images, the humans escaped to the shore, taking what they could from the ship, then the ship sank, which is when it damaged their dome. The sea dragons, who call themselves Ragurans, hauled the ship to a crevice in the seafloor away from their home, but the ship was still alive then. And it's still alive today. The reactor in it is still functioning, although it is damaged and streaming radiation into the sea. This is what is convoluting the sea life and making the water on Erinnua unsafe for the humans here."

There, he'd said his piece, and he breathed easier for it. He could only hope the governor would believe him although, at the moment, the man's face had gone quite still with an unreadable expression on it. Dari glanced at Grania, who dipped her head in a little nod of approval before she looked toward the authority again. Liam cleared his throat with a "humph" sound as they waited for a reaction.

The governor blinked a few times as if he was waking up from a dream, then said, "Well, that is quite a story, lad. Frankly, I am disinclined to believe it. However, these fine folks, from the O'Ceagan clan have supported your tale, so it must have some merit. Have you any proof?"

Dari hesitated, considering how much he could actually tell him without revealing his true self. "I have seen the reactor with me own eyes, sir. And I told the captain here about it, gave her the specifics of what I had seen. She took it back to Liam, her engineer, and he identified the reactor that I saw. It matches up with one that was on the ship that came here from Earth. The only other proof I can offer would be a twisted, distorted fish from the sea."

"Photos or videos of this would have been helpful," the government man said in a condescending tone.

Well, Dari figured he could hardly tell him that he didn't have a human body under the sea to hold a recording device.

At that point, Liam spoke up. "The reactor he has described in detail matches a Trident model that was used at the launch time. There is a scarcity of information about the fate of the ship that brought the settlers here. I can't help but wonder why that is. When I thought about this, I realized we were taught very little about the actual landing when I was in school."

"What Liam says is true," Trigg added. "As little children, we were always told not to go in the water or drink any water unless it came from the home's purified supply or was bottled. That it wasn't safe for people to drink or be in. But no one ever said why that was so. Do you know anything about it, sir?"

The governor shifted in his seat, and he fidgeted with a writing implement on the desk. "I heard the same warnings when I was growing up, and no one explained anything then either. It's something that my parents were taught by their parents and so on back through the generations here on our world. I did hear, when I was in the master class, a story or a rumor that something bad had happened when the ship landed, so it is possible."

"I think we need to find out," Grania said. She leaned forward in her chair. "We'd like to take a shuttle out to the location that Dari has pinpointed to see what is there. Our scanners can detect if the ship is down there, and an environment suit would protect one of us if we went down to the crevice to explore and get those videos you asked about. We just need your permission to do it."

He shuffled his tablet around the desk and tapped at it, calling up information, Dari assumed. He looked at the puca again. "I still don't understand, Mr. Dari, how you could have seen all this. Did you have a diving suit?"

Well, now, how do I answer this? Maybe telling him the truth wouldn't be such a shock after all if Grania has already told the man he was fae.

Instead, Dari said, "No, I do not, but I can breathe underwater, you see."

As soon as he said it, Dari realized that the governor clearly did not see. His jaw dropped open, and he peered at him like the puca was a stranger beast than he'd perceived. And that was without seeing his true form. "You can do what?"

"He means he has an air tank," Grania said before Dari could reply. "He can breathe underwater through it, but the dive is rather deep to make without a suit, and you have to be very careful."

Dari shifted his eyes to the floor, studying the pattern of interlocked rings on the carpeting before he ventured a glance at Liam, who was barely containing a laugh. In that moment, it became quite apparent that the fae remark didn't mean that the governor understood he was a sidhe and could shift shapes. Still, if it proved necessary to tell him and change before his very eyes in order to get the problem taken care of, then he was prepared to do it.

Grania's explanation appeared to mollify the man although he turned a stern look at Dari and said, "Even though you are a recent arrival on Erinnua, you should be aware of our laws. You broke them by going into the water when the law is there to protect the people. You may fall ill from having done so, and you'd best be seeing a physician to determine if your health is compromised. I will not be levying any charges against you for your transgression, but unless the law can be lifted, you should avoid the lakes, seas, rivers, and drinking any of the polluted water."

"What about our request?" Liam asked, bringing them back to the reason they'd asked for an audience.

"Yes, that," he said. "Well, I need to do a little research and studying on this before I can say if you should pursue any action. I will get back to you in a week or so."

With that, he dismissed them. No specific answer to their request, just a promise to respond, whether it be good or bad. Dari's shoulders slumped with the realization it may be weeks before they could do anything.

As they strolled back toward the transport, Liam said, "Don't you look so glum, Dari. He says he'll look into it and consider it. Now we wait for the decision. If he doesn't agree that it needs to be cleaned up, then we take it to a higher authority."

"There's a higher authority for the planet?" Dari asked. He'd thought they had been talking to the highest one, so the remark surprised him.

"Oh, yes," Grania said. "If we have to, we can take it all the way to the Dragon Council, which has authority for all the inhabited planets in the Dragon Star system. If we believe there is a danger to Erinnua and its inhabitants, then the council can take action, asking that the problem be neutralized or resolved, or they will ban visitors to the planet and exports from it. That would put a major financial embargo here that would not be good for any of us."

"That would make matters worse, then," Dari said, not understanding how this would help.

"True, it would. But it would never get that far. It's a way to pressure the planet's government to resolve the problem."

He started to get the picture, and so he began to learn more about how the star system's government worked.

*****

As it turned out, the governor sent a message to Grania within two days giving her the go-ahead to survey the area of the damage, take videos, get water samples, and present a plan to rectify the situation.

Bringing the news to Sheilan and Dari, the captain grinned as she read the words to them and explained what they would do. "You did well, Dari. This is a great start. Now we can get the shuttle out, and you can join Liam and Trigg with the survey and scans. This gives you the authorization to go into the water while working on this problem. However, the governor would also like images of the Ragurans, and some kind of authorization for what we would be doing. You're going to have to visit them again, explain the situation, and get their permission."

That alarmed Dari more than a little. The last time he had tried to talk to Gradifin, the sea dragon had tried to kill him. Even Alia seemed opposed to allowing humans anywhere near their colony or in their sea if they could prevent it. How was he going to convince them that the humans would not cause more damage?

Seeing his worried expression, Grania asked, "Is that a problem?"

"It may be. They are understandably nervous about humans coming back into the water and the possibility of more damage. They have not been too open to the suggestion when I've approached them."

"That could throw a spanner in the stardrive if they aren't cooperative." Her frown made him feel as if he'd let her down.

"Give me a couple of days, and I will go see them again and try to get the urgency of it through to them. Sometimes the language of telepathy is hard to show ideas and things to repair a problem. Can we survey before we have their approval or will this delay that?"

Grania read the message again, then shrugged her shoulders. "He doesn't say specifically if we have to have approval while we're assessing the damage, but we will need it before we can take any action."

"Then let's proceed with the first part," Dari suggested. "I will find an approach to presenting it so that they understand that the engine is more dangerous to them than the humans."

"I agree. Liam suggested you fellows do it tomorrow. He has a little time, and Trigg is also free, so it's a good time to get this done. It won't interfere with the Ragurans, so you don't need to worry about convincing them before then, but you could warn them that the shuttle will be out there and not to worry." Grania tapped a message into her communicator, likely to confirm it to Liam.

With that much settled, the captain took her leave saying she was heading back to the space station to check on her ship. Sheilan had said very little during this meeting, remaining quiet and petting the kitcoon, for the most part. Dari turned to her now.

"So, what are you thinking, bean sidhe? Do you still think I am going outside the scope of what is accepted by the Council?"

She barely looked up at him. "As long as I am not involved in it, Dari, then the council has no issue with me so far as you are concerned other than bringing you to this planet. You, on the other hand, are beholden to no one, not to the humans, the sea dragons, or the Sidhe Council. Of all the folk, you are the most independent and were created that way, so if you choose to do this, what can they say?"

"Then why did you argue against it?" Dari leaned against the tree and looked down at her.

"Because it is my nature, and I wished you to consider what you were about to do. I hear you almost revealed yourself to the governor. That could have been dangerous." She glanced up at him, her right eyebrow lifting in an unasked question.

"I almost did, and I would have if it was necessary to convince him. I would still do it if he decides not to continue this through." The puca felt the risk was worth it.

"Would you show him your true nature, puca?"

He knelt down to her eye level, stared straight into them, and said, "I would. If I needed to reduce to my energy form, I would do that. What could he do to me? Lock me up? He'd have to catch a speeding ball of light, and I would just escape, even if he could."

"Such serious thoughts," Sheilan said, tilting her head a little and regarding him with her own intense stare. "I think I might be rubbing off on you. You never used to care much about any of the life you played your tricks on. Why now?"

"Because it affects me, too! I am fond of the water. My water horse yearns to get out and romp in the lakes and sea. But that thing is a danger to me also. It has already created a problem for me."

"And?" she prompted.

"And I don't want to see the life on this planet threatened by an unseen danger. Liam said that if it remained running and the waters aren't treated, it could affect this world for hundreds of years or more. They are fortunate that the humans haven't mutated already. Can you not see the danger here?"

"Of course, I can. I also can see the danger if the government becomes aware of sidhe in their midst. I do not think that telling them they only have two of us here, or better yet, one of us, would make them regard us any less of threat. We are alien to them.

While their Irish ancestors welcomed some of our kind, they feared others. With good reason. Those stories may live on with these people, and they might devise a trap that can hold us captive."

"I doubt that. We can move through anything."

"Are you forgetting the targassium crystal, Dari?" Her voice took on a dark tone.

He shuddered as he recalled the unpolished crystal with all its raw power that nearly drained his life energy. It had been smuggled on board the ship on the way here. Neither Sheilan nor he knew if it could kill them, but it had proved frightening enough to have been so depleted. Feeling a little shaky at the thought of it, he shook his head.

"There might be more powerful things in the universe, my friend," Sheilan went on. "'Tis best not to assume that nothing can harm us."

Dari had to agree with that thought. Now, he turned his thoughts to how he could convince the sea dragons that the humans would not do more damage and the fact was, he did not know for sure that was true. While he had a lot of faith in Captain Grania and her brother, this wasn't something they had dealt with before.

CHAPTER 14

First Steps to Resolution

Having decided on the best approach, Dari ambled down to the seashore closest to the dome, which was still at least a couple of miles across the water. Close enough to put out a tentative contact to Alia, he hoped he would be able to reach her. He asked her to communicate with him, no easy thing to convey in images. But he stood on the shore and repeated it frequently as he waited for over a hundred mites to detect a response of any kind.

After not getting anything, he decided he would need to go look for her, stripped off his clothes, and waded into the water. Ducking his head under, he dove into a wave and swam forward to the deeper water, ready to change into the water horse, when he spotted Alia only a half dozen feet from him. She pulled up, her body going upright and ready to protect herself as those faceted eyes focused on the naked human body she saw in front of her.

Dari mind-spoke to her then to tell her he was a friend and not to fear him. Her body tensed while her tail whipped around. He changed forms in front of her, switching to the water horse form that she'd first seen. If anything, the change appeared to frighten her more. At that moment, Dari realized she'd never actually seen him switch, only the form after the transformation had been completed.

I be Dari, he told her in symbols.

How? she responded. She lowered her guard a little, accepting his voice.

I change forms. You see me as this one before. You see me as sea dragon. The first is my human form. He didn't think the explanation helped.

What are you? Her rigid body reflected her apprehension and her barbed tail lifted in readiness of a battle.

It was a fair question. Seeing this from Alia's perspective, he would be as curious and wary about himself as she was.

I am – He faltered for an image or a word she would understand to convey his pure energy form as a sidhe.

She sent him an image that he thought resembled a demon.

No… Not evil, he managed to send back, and added an image of a ghost or spirit, if that meant anything to her.

Her tail lowered, but she stayed a safe distance from him. Using what little Dari knew of her language, he told her that he and the humans that he trusted would be coming out to the gorge where the bad ship rested to figure out how to shut it down.

He sensed her panic as soon as he got the message across. He countered with what he understood of the danger. Images from his mind showed her what might happen to all of them and the planet if the reactor continued to function. He could sense the alarm in her and the fear.

You trust hua-mans? she asked. The alien word didn't form easily in her mind.

Not all. But ones who will fix this, I do. They be wise and skilled. Dari hoped he got the words right to convey his confidence in Grania and her brothers.

Gradifin no like.

Dari rocked in acknowledgment, then asked, *Gradifin –mate?*

You mean make little dragons? No. Not matched yet.

He took that to mean that she hadn't been paired with anyone and Gradifin had no claim on her. Yet he acted as if he did.

Alia must have picked up on that thought somehow because she added, *Gradifin be family. We have same egg-layer.*

You mean mother? Same parents? he shot back. Then he be your brother.

She confirmed with an image of large sea dragon eggs hatching and little ones swimming out.

Your brother, he repeated.

Using this back and forth image and emotion sort-of-speaking, Dari managed to convey to her that he needed to explain everything to the Ragurans. If it meant that Gradifin had to approve, then he needed to talk to him without him thinking Dari was the enemy. Once he got that across, she told him to wait, and she would relay the message to him. If Gradifin agreed, she would bring him back to see Dari. If not or if he could not come now, then she would mind speak to him. Once he indicated that he understood, she was off, her powerful body zipping like an arrow through the water.

Dari lingered in the water, swimming in ever-growing circles while waiting for an answer. Now that he knew the problem, he felt less comfortable in the environment. While he wanted to help Alia and her people, the truth came down to his own need to be able to enjoy the waters on Erinnua. If he and Liam's team couldn't neutralize the threat, he couldn't remain on this planet.

After what seemed like a long time as Dari noted the shifting underwater shading from the sun's progress, he finally felt a mind tickle and focused on Alia's voice. *Gradifin not come now. Will try to tell him. I contact you later.*

That was it for the day then, he conceded as he swam back to the shore and transformed to the lad again. Slipping back into his clothes, he checked to make sure no other damage altered his pattern and was relieved that nothing more seemed missing or different.

*****

Dari peered out the shuttle window as it skimmed over the water about twenty feet above it on a fine, clear day.

"'Tis a good day for checking out the area," Liam said as he brought the shuttle to a hover over the open area that Dari had guided him to using his mental map from his last visit.

Dari couldn't explain exactly how his vision worked except to say that he saw everything in precise forms that he could picture when he looked at the zone. Key markers on the shore gave him a clear positioning sense.

Liam's friend Trigg leaned out the open door, gazing down at the dark, almost purple water as if he might see the deadly reactor's glow gleaming through it.

"It's down there," Dari told him. "About two hundred feet below us."

Liam set the shuttle to hold the position, then moved to the fancy-looking equipment in the back. Big screens and a charting device sat alongside a computer console to control it. A third-dimension printer sat to the port side of the machine. He turned on the computer and keyed in coordinates as he explained the procedure to Dari.

"This instrument will scan a section of the sea below us and draw a three-dimensional map of the ocean floor, as well as the ship in the gorge once we find it. I expect it to take a little while to pinpoint the exact spot where you saw it, Dari. But once we do, we'll see exactly what it's like down there."

"Pardon my ignorance," Dari said. "But why was this not

done before?"

His eyes got that blank, uncertain look that humans sometimes exhibited when asked a question they hadn't considered previously. "What do you mean?"

"The ocean and seas of Earth are well-mapped, photographed, and made into representations for people to use for navigation. They have been for centuries, millennia even. Why did no one here do the same thing?"

"Oh, I get what you're saying now." He tapped a button on the screen, and the machine started mapping the area, a low hum coming from it just to let them know it was working. "Well, I guess that it's because our people were forbidden to go into the seas, so there seemed to be no reason to do it. We don't even sail ships here. All inter-island transport is by shuttles that fly well above the water."

"So no one's ever questioned the ban or even tried sailing in the lakes?" It seemed incredible to the puca that none of these people, who came from a race of humans who made their living from the oceans, never once had the urge to go on the water.

Liam glanced at the scanner image as Trigg began checking the flat map the machine spewed to the tablet he held in front of him. "When you grow up being told that the water is dangerous and will kill you, then only a few are foolhardy enough to go into it."

"And you would be one of them," Trigg crowed, grinning at his mate.

"Only once and not very far out," Liam responded, narrowing his eyes in an unspoken reprimand to the other man. "My skin felt blistered for several days afterward, and I had to lie to me dad about how I'd gotten that outrageous burn."

"So, you have seen the distorted plants and fishes under the waves," Dari stated. "You knew what I said was the truth."

"That I did, Dari-boy. But I never saw any of the sea dragons you spoke of so they must not come close-in to the shores." He smiled at Dari, then returned his eyes to the controls to nudge the shuttle to the next zone.

They repeated this scan-and-move process another two times without turning up anything that resembled the ship, but on the fourth try, Trigg's keen eyes caught something on the screen, just to the west of their position. "Look at that rise of seafloor there. It's a sudden build up compared to the area around it."

Liam leaned over to look, then peered at the scanner again. "I'm thinking…"

"That it's from displacement," Trigg interjected. "When the Ragurans moved the ship, they probably dragged it to the crevice and an object that size – "

"Would leave a large rut in the sand," Liam finished, their minds working together in that way two old friends could do.

"So, what are you saying?" Dari asked.

"That the ship is probably a short way off to the northwest," Liam answered and dashed forward to move the shuttle again.

As soon as the scans started coming in from the new section, the images looked different. Then they saw the first section of the broken ship.

"There it is," Trigg shouted and pointed to the scanner where the irregular tube-shape came into view.

"Fated fairies, that's a big ship," Liam remarked as more of it became visible.

He eased the shuttle forward until the broken lower section was revealed, and they could see the details of the engine and the reactor. Another piece of equipment came to life recording more information.

"Radiation readout," Liam said, "and the amounts are climbing rapidly. Holy Mother, look at these numbers! And you were down there next to this, Dari?"

"I was," he answered. "Very nearly killed the form I was wearing." Trigg raised an eyebrow as Dari said that.

"You really can shift shapes?" he asked, a definite tone of disbelief in his voice.

The puca gave him a hard stare, one not usually associated with his easy-going human form, and said, "I'm doing it right now, laddie." Even his voice dropped to a deeper, more menacing tone.

Trigg held up a hand, palm open. "Just asking. No harm meant."

Liam chuckled. "Careful, Trigg. It doesn't pay to piss off a puca."

His friend nodded and turned his attention back to the scans and readings. "I think we'll be getting enough data to figure out how bad the situation is and allow us to look at what we can do to neutralize it once the reactor is shut down."

"The images of the reactor and the rest of the engine are coming in pretty clearly, but we need to get video of it so we can see exactly how it sits and what problems we might encounter shutting it down," Liam said.

Dari shuddered at the prospect, but managed to volunteer anyway. "I can take a camera down and get the recording if you show me how it works and can lower it down to me once I'm in the water."

He figured the dragon form, which had fingers of a sort, should be able to manipulate a camera. Even though the pattern had been damaged and might come out of this even worse, it was the best he had for going in the water. After the last experience, he had to be concerned about erasing more of his base pattern, but he counted it worth the risk.

"Send you down in that radiation, Dari?" Liam said. "I don't think so. It's not necessary for any of us to go in the water at this time. We have a robotic camera on board for this purpose. We can control it from here, and it will record everything. It will be able to get much closer than you could get without killing your form."

Dari breathed a sigh of relief. "That's good then. I did not look forward to it."

He watched as Liam and Trigg readied the camera robot, a piece of equipment that resembled a large egg with two fins and a blade rotor at the back. The front section housed the camera, which fit in the nose section behind a clear transparent plasti-steel dome, as Liam called it. It looked like curved glass to the puca. Trigg checked the remote control and nodded his head in satisfaction as the camera clicked on.

Then they sealed the unit, and Trigg and Liam lowered it into the water on a platform from the shuttle and turned on the engine. Shooting away from the platform, the little unit went down into the water and disappeared from view, but Trigg watched its progress through the camera lens transmission to his tablet.

This modern technology fascinated Dari, so he questioned Liam who patiently explained anything he did not understand. Even though he had been alive all the time that the world was growing and developing all this modern stuff, Dari had not acquired any direct contact or knowledge with it for most of that time. Even the spaceships remained a mystery to him, although he and Sheilan learned quite a bit on the voyage here.

"So, what do we do now?" Dari asked, not at all certain what the next step would be. He still had to convince the Ragurans, and that loomed ahead of him in the next two days. But once that was done, he had no idea.

Liam tore his eyes away from the image he was watching on a monitor screen. "We, which is to say, Trigg and I, will review the images, look at the data we've collected and get together with a couple of experts at the space station to figure out the best approach to shutting that reactor down and sealing the ship away. My best guess is that we'll set off a series of explosions that will collapse the sides of the gorge into it to fill it in. Then, we'll see if we have any way to neutralize the radiation down to a safe level."

"What about me? What am I to be doing while you're up on the station doing that?"

"You still have to convince the sea dragons that this is for their own good. Once we have the plan, then you, with their help, will have to warn any sea creatures to stay away from the area on the day we decide we'll do it. But the plan will need to be completely approved by the governor's advisors, so it may be a few days or a few weeks until we have the approval."

"A few weeks?" Dari questioned with a sinking feeling in his stomach. "That's a long time."

"It is," he agreed, "but not so long when you consider how long ago this thing happened. Once we have the go ahead, we gather up what we need, get the shuttle, and head out to this spot again to do it."

"Will I be part of that job?" Dari asked. He felt like he was being cut out of all of it.

"You will," Liam answered. "You're still our best guide to this area, and you are the only one who's been down there. We'll need to see if we can find an environment suit to fit you though. Most of them are larger than you."

"I have an adult form I could use," Dari said, although he wasn't sure that the old harper would be the ideal form to use for traipsing around the sea bottom.

"That's good to know." Liam turned his attention back to the screen and said, "I think it's time to bring it back home, Trigg. We should have everything we need from every angle."

As Trigg directed the camera 'bot back to the shuttle's lowered platform, Liam began copying and transmitting all the data they'd collected to the space station and the Mo Croidhe's computers.

At least, Dari could report to the Ragurans that the first step of fixing the situation was done, and the humans were working on it. While it didn't seem like much, every problem had a starting point. It would be up to the underwater residents if they proceeded once they had the approval.

And he still needed to get photos or images of the Ragurans to prove they existed. He'd talked to Liam about that, and he'd given Dari a tiny recording device he could attach to his underwater form if he could figure out how to do that.

If he took the sea dragon form, he had a hand with taloned fingers that he could use to manipulate the device. But he would undoubtedly rile up Gradifin, which would be disastrous. His water horse, on the other hand, had hooves, which didn't give him anything to use to attach the camera once he transformed. Perhaps Sheilan could help him out.

CHAPTER 15

Two Steps Forward

Dari dragon-paddled, if that's what one could call what he did with his awkward arms and flippers wiggling to stay in one place, in the central green of the main section where most of the Ragurans had their homes or caves or whatever they called them. Just about everyone, including a few strays who lived outside the dome, had come out to listen to what he had to say. Alia and her brother had done an excellent job of communicating the urgency of his request to them.

As Dari looked at the assembled group, less than a hundred of them, he realized that even the little ones were included, some sea dragons still just infant-sized but paddling along with the rest of them. After consultation with Sheilan and more telepathic conversing with Alia, he had assumed his slightly battered sea dragon form that no longer resembled Gradifin as closely as it had. When he had explained the necessity of wearing it, not only for being able to manipulate the camera but to give an image of familiarity to the other Ragurans. They had agreed it would make him more acceptable to all of them if he looked like the same species.

Now, he worried about communicating with them and being able to get the whole story across, but Alia devised a plan to make it easier. Dari would be open only to her communication, a relatively simple step for him to block out all other thought links that might be in the area and focus only on hers. She would be the conduit, receiving any comments and relaying them to him in the thought-language they had already established. His presentation would be filtered through her, and she would rephrase it, as good a word as any, to terms and images they would understand.

So, Dari began after Gradifin explained he was from another part of the world and that he had news that was important to them. Then he added that Alia would be interpreting for Dari, and they seemed to accept that with no concerns.

Moving into the middle of the circle, Dari touched first on their history, the ship crashing to the oceans and the people on board. He told them the strangers were humans from the planet Earth and gave them a brief history of their world. He made it clear that the humans didn't intend to harm any of the Ragurans and did not know of their existence until recently. That caused a bit of a stir since he had not realized that they were not aware of the humans on the surface. In retrospect, it made sense if they never went out of the water or close enough to the shore to see them.

He then explained about the reactor in the ship and that what it produced and leaked into their water was having ill effects on them. That opened the door to questions. Did it make them sick? Was it responsible for their low population and why they had trouble having little ones? Why so many of their eggs did not reach maturity? Why some of them grew twisted?

The questions went on and on, and Alia did her best to answer them as did Dari. Eventually, he had her tell them, *Truth is, I do not have all answers. Bad machine is not good for health of Ragurans or any sea life or humans on planet.*

An odd buzz assaulted his senses at that statement, and Dari realized they were doing a kind of keening of anxiety or grief. He wasn't sure what. When he looked to Alia, he saw she was making the odd noise along with them.

When it stopped, she tried to explain. *They pray to Ranuvara, the source of life, for help. This frightens my people.*

I bring hope. Tell them.

She did, and they turned hundreds of faceted eyes toward Dari, waiting for their miracle to be delivered, it would seem. He went on to explain the plan to them and let them know that humans wanted to clean up the problem that their ancestors caused.

Then came the harder part, asking them for permission to allow the humans to shut down the reactor and bury the whole ship in the ravine where they had dragged it. It took Alia several tries to explain it in terms they understood. Then they asked questions and voiced objections. He answered the best he could with his limited knowledge of what Liam was actually going to do.

Finally, he ended with giving them a grim picture of what it might be like in a few more generations with the ultimate destruction the ship could still cause them and the other life on the planet. Dari didn't want to tell them that if they said no, eventually the humans would do it anyway and kill anything that got in their way. He had enough experience of human nature to know they would get their way in the long run.

His plea completed, Alia led Dari away to a cave and told him to wait there while her people debated this and made their decision. After she left, he explored the spacious area that had several large shelves protruding from the back wall that he presumed they used as beds or resting couches. Each looked large enough to accommodate a sea dragon bigger than Gradifin. The cave itself seemed to be made of limestone or something similar that could be easily carved and shaped. As to any other amenities, he could find none. They lived in the sea and presumably had few needs except a secure place to rest. In that way, they were like Sheilan and him. All they needed was their dirt.

He stretched his alien body out on one of the lower platforms and relaxed, finding it comfortable. He might have even dozed off for a little bit until he heard Alia's thought-voice calling him. Her form filled the opening to the cave, and she beckoned to him with her arms.

When he followed her back to the central green, he noted the crowd had broken into seven smaller groups. Then they cast their votes to either approve or reject the plan. The groups, it turned out, were family units, and they voted as a family. One by one, a representative came forward and declared for the family. The first two in favor, the next opposed. The one after that nervously agreeing to the plan, and another one saying no, then another negative vote.

The last vote came from Gradifin, who voted for his small family of five that included his mate, their two offspring, and his sister. Dari held his breath. If he voted no, the plan would not proceed. How much did he dislike Dari and the humans? Enough to deny them an opportunity to make things right and doom his race along with the rest of the sea?

He swam up to Dari, shot a hard look at him, and he could almost see his body, which was Gradifin's form, reflected in the facets of the sea dragon's eyes. In spite of Dari's selective blocking, his mind-voice came through. *I not trust humans, but I trust Dari. If you say good, my clan votes yes.*

Dari felt his heart thumping as relief shot through his body. *I do trust the humans I will be working alongside, and I will make sure it is done right.*

To his surprise, Gradifin raised a taloned hand toward him in friendship, and he offered his in return. The sea dragon pressed his hand against the puca's, locking his fingers around Dari's for a moment, then released it. He turned and swam away with his family, the rest of the Ragurans following behind him.

Dari felt the touch of Alia's mind. *Do not fail us, Dari.*

Then she swam with him to the dome exit.

As he left them behind, Dari felt a heavy responsibility he was not used to feeling. Pucas did not care about the problems of others. Yet, now he did.

*****

A few days later, Liam, Trigg, and Brendan dropped by to see Dari without first sending a message. The puca lingered above a branch in the tree above the soil plot that the humans called Moira's Grave even though only a little of her rested in the dirt Sheilan and he had brought. In his energy form, he couldn't be seen easily as he floated above a leaf-filled twig.

Liam called out for him as if he expected him to be nearby and in human form. With a wicked thought, Dari zipped from the tree to the nearby bushes and changed to his horse form. Not the sturdy but short hill pony he often wore, but the full-fledged, sixteen-hands white horse with demon red eyes. He let out a whinny and trotted from the cover into plain sight, then reared up and held it with front legs striking out in fighting fashion.

Liam's eyes bugged out in surprise and Brendan jumped back a couple of feet behind his older brother. Trigg's mouth fell open before he ran back several feet and stared at Dari as if he had seen a ghost or something. Now, Liam had seen his smaller horse visage before, and Brendan knew he took on the form, even though the lad wasn't quite sure what a horse was, but Dari's horse was a totally unknown creature to Trigg.

He thumped his legs down in front of them and kicked up the hind legs in a move that would frighten anyone standing behind him. And sure enough, someone was behind him, but not so close as to make contact. Fortunate for him.

"Dari! Behave yourself," Sheilan called out. "We have visitors."

He grumbled in horse terms with a sort of whickering noise, then settled on all fours and trotted back to the bushes. After he changed to his human form and found his clothes to put on, Dari strolled out to greet them.

Sheilan had invited them into their living room, which amounted to sitting under the tree.

Liam spotted him first and waved, saying, "That was an impressive display, Dari. Is that the form you used on the pirate's ship?"

"It is," he replied.

"Well, I can see why that frightened the blazes out of them," Brendan added.

On the other hand, Trigg avoided looking at Dari. In a tense, slightly annoyed voice, he asked, "What the hell was that?"

"'Tis called a horse," the puca replied. "An Earth animal."

"It's a frightening creature, but what kind of welcome was that to give friends?"

"'Twas just a little prank. No harm. I thought you might like to see what a puca can do."

"Scare people?" He brought his eyes to Dari, an angry glare glistening in them.

"Sometimes." He sat himself down next to Sheilan and caught the sly smile that Brendan flashed at him. Perhaps Trigg was not high on the lad's list of favorite people.

"So, what has brought you to our place?" Dari asked.

"We think we have a plan, and we want to show you what we've got. But it looks like you haven't got a table here. What do you say we go down to the family house and take over our dining room there?"

The O'Ceagan farmhouse sat about a half-mile from their plot, but Shielan and Dari had never been invited there. Grania and her brothers had kept their existence a secret from the rest of the O'Ceagan family.

He glanced at Sheilan, who gave him a nod. "Take care while you're there and mind your manners." It was her way of warning him to not change forms in front of the household. While this small group knew what he was, it would not do to let the whole family know, although he personally thought that it would come out eventually.

As it happened, the house was mostly empty with only the boys' great granda there. The old man was preoccupied with a project of his own, so he barely acknowledged they were there. Settling at the table, Brendan pulled out his tablet and rolled out a three-foot by five-foot screen that looked like a mat on the wooden surface, then he connected his tablet with a tap and called up an image of the ship in the crevice. All leaning in to see the picture, they got down to business.

Liam pointed to the reactor and started talking about the type it was and what it would take to turn it off. The governor, he told them, had opened some sealed records from the landing and found some information on the crash. "The crew reported that they couldn't disable the reactor, so they abandoned it, and allowed it to fill with water and sink. They believed the reactor would burn out in a few years, and they agreed to not tell the rest of the immigrants any of the details except to declare the water on the planet unsafe to go in or drink untreated."

"That was irresponsible on their part," Brendan said before Dari could make a similar remark. "How could they justify keeping this from their leadership?"

Liam shrugged. "I don't have any answers, little brother. That was the only information I had from the sealed records. The ship was damaged, landed in the water, and the engines malfunctioned. They were stuck here until they got a foothold and could build new ships."

"Makes you wonder what else the authorities have held back from us," Trigg commented. "If I recall from our history, the Earth Space Agency had checked out the viable planets to support life in the Dragon system. They would have noted if there was a problem with the water quality."

"Absolutely," Brendan agreed. "I read that also. The ship had over three thousand immigrants plus two hundred crew, if I recall, so why did no one question why the water was unsafe?"

"Why didn't we ask when we heard about it?" Liam countered. "We just accepted it as the way things were and went on with our business. Maybe the settlers thought the ESA had made a mistake."

"You can be discussing it all you want," Dari said, "but the real issue now is how do we fix it?"

"Quite right, Dari," Liam replied. "Now, with the information we have in our database on this reactor, there are three ways we can approach a shut-down on it. The most obvious one is to power it down through the computers, which were probably not working and are totally destroyed by now. This would have been the way the crew tried, so that is not viable."

"Anyone hungry?" Brendan asked out of the blue.

Liam shot a look at him.

"What? I missed breakfast, and my distraught stomach is leaning against my spine for support. I'm going to raid the kitchen." He sprang to his feet and started toward the archway that separated the two rooms.

"Bring back something to drink," Liam called as he shook his head at his youngest brother. "Kid's always hungry."

Then he made the picture on his screen bigger and pointed to a connector leading to the reactor. "This is another way to shut it down. First, we need to cut off the fuel supply. It looks like it's been pulling sea water into it through a stuck input valve, so we need to close that first, then we can access the power generator and turn it off." He went on to detail more of what he and Trigg would need to do.

In the middle of it, Brendan came back in with a platter of food that included, fruit, cheese, and a loaf of soda bread in one hand and a pitcher of cold cider in the other. Dari's mouth watered at the sight. It had been a long time since he had eaten any soda bread.

"Oh, my man, that looks great," Trigg said as he eyed the platter of food.

Within minutes, they were all reaching for something to munch on. Dari stabbed a piece of cheese and cut a slice of the bread, then settled back to feast on this plowman's lunch that Brendan had found. The taste was heavenly bringing back memories of the last time Dari had been in this form in Ireland. While the pub food he had eaten on this world had been good, it had been lacking in the simplicity of Irish bread and cheese.

Liam poured a glass of the cider for each of them, which proved to be as good as any apple cider Dari had ever tasted. "This here is a very fine brew," he said as he raised a glass in thanks. "Did ya bring it back from Ireland?"

"Not at all," he replied. "'Tis from our own trees. Apples and pears are two of the trees the settlers brought from Earth that adapted easily to the soil and climate here."

They were feeling a little more mellow now, and even Trigg seemed more relaxed around the puca. Dari picked up the sharp pointed knife and made a stab for another piece of cheese at the exact same moment that Brendan came at it with a fork. In just the time of a snap of a finger, their hands collided and Dari sliced the edge of Brendan's hand while he stabbed the puca's. Not badly hurt, mind you, but enough that Bren was bleeding quite a bit.

"Fecking fairies!" Brendan swore as he jerked his hand back, which made it worse.

A fair amount oozed out from Dari's hand also, but he was more concerned about Brendan's cut that was dripping onto the tray of food. Dari grabbed a linen napkin and pressed it against Bren's wound with his own bloody hand.

Seeing that Dari had that part under control, Liam dashed off for a med kit.

"Sorry about that, boy-o," Dari said, which, given that he looked younger than the other lad, caused both Brendan and Trigg to cast odd looks at him.

"Me, also," Brendan answered. "I guess we were both too focused on the cheese." He flashed a grin at Dari that spoke of the fine Irish charm that the lad possessed.

"I'll take care of it in a minute," Liam said as he returned, opened the med kit, and pulled out a tube of Insta-Stitch and a sealing pen. In no time, he'd cleaned Brendan's wound, then glued and sealed it. He turned to Dari next, but sidhe that he was, his poked holes were already nearly healed.

Excitement over, they cleaned up the table and Liam poured

another round of cider before they got back to the business of how they were going to seal the gorge once the reactor was shut down.

"Explosive charges, placed here, here, here, and here," Trigg said as he marked them around the edge of the opening and just below the rims. "The angle we place them will cause the sides to cave in and cover the ship. Dari, you'll need to be sure the Ragurans and any other sea animals stay clear of the area, so none are accidentally hurt or killed."

"That's my job, then? Nothing with actually shutting it down?" Disappointment slumped his shoulders. He felt so excluded after all the planning. How could he be sure the job was done right if he wasn't in the thick of it?

"Not totally," Liam answered. "We may need your help with a few things so long as we can find an environment suit to fit you. Is your harper form about Brendan's size or shorter?"

"Shorter," Dari said right off. Brendan was almost as tall as Liam although not as muscular, being still just a lad.

"How about Nansi or Grania?" he asked next.

"Closer to the captain. Maybe a little shorter, but not much."

"The suit adjusts a bit, so hers will probably work. We'll bring it along."

That settled, the meeting broke up and Dari bid farewell as the lads took their shuttle back to the port. Feeling somewhat tired, he cast a look around and didn't see anyone in the area, so he changed forms, and flew home.

CHAPTER 16

An Awkward Problem

As Dari emerged from the soil a few hours later, he realized something felt different. He had a new pattern shining in his essence. How? He puzzled over it, but then he realized what had happened. Curious, he reached for the recently-added design and began to fill it in, building the form from the nearby molecules, reshaping them as needed. After almost ten minutes—new constructs always took time—Dari had completed the form and he stared at the hands, arms, and legs of the tall, slender human he had created. He made his way to a pond that wasn't far from the hill, and in the last fading light of the day, he beheld his new form and face in the water.

Dark-haired, blue-eyed, and a handsome young fellow, Dari looked exactly like Brendan O'Ceagan. He studied the reflection for almost a full minute until he realized the new body mimicked the lad exactly. No breaks in the pattern, no mismatched eyes, no slightly turned wrong feet, but a perfect replica.

Shocked, he stepped back and ran his hands over his face. He didn't believe it at first as he had not eaten any of Brendan to get the pattern, so finally, he concluded that it had been his blood. When it had fallen on Dari's injured hand, some had flowed into his wound and stayed in his blood, which then passed it to his energy sphere to record the pattern. And, being the first pattern Dari had taken since he had been at the reactor, he'd created

Brendan's form whole and unblemished.

Naked and a bit worried, Dari sat cross-legged on the grass to consider what he'd done. What did he do now? Set the form aside and never use it, not letting anyone know about it? It could be useful, and it would fit one of the environment suits easier than his harper form would, not to mention Brendan's body was stronger and more suited to the job. How would the lad feel about having a duplicate that was a puca? Worse, what would Captain Grania think?

He shivered a little as the evening settled in with a chill and the moon began to rise over the sea. One thing for sure, if he chose to use the body, he'd need to get more clothing. He released the form to return to his sidhe spirit and floated like a will-o-the-wisp back to the home tree.

Sheilan seemed less than impressed when Dari related the whole incident to her. Her eyes narrowed as she frowned at him.

"You just cannot stay out of trouble, can you, puca?"

"I did not do it on purpose," he protested, leaning back against the tree in Brendan's form, his legs crossed to try to maintain some sense of decorum in the presence of the bean sidhe. "'Twas entirely an accident and the thought had not even crossed me mind. I'm as surprised as anyone that this happened."

"You need clothes, Dari. You cannot sit around like that in the open as we are right now."

"Perhaps you could acquire some from Brendan?" he suggested.

"I will not," she argued. "'Tis bad enough you've done it. I am not about to go asking the lad for clothes. I will find some in town. Now change back to your boy form before someone sees you. What was his name anyway?"

"I think he called himself Lugh or something like that."

Dari complied, vanishing to switch forms and put on some clothing. He wished he had the ability to create garments with the body as Sheilan did, but it seemed the goddess deemed it not necessary for pucas. Likely, she never expected one of them to take a human form.

When Dari returned, Sheilan stared at him for a long minute and arched an eyebrow. "You are back to normal."

"I am back to this form, yes."

"I mean that you are the same as you were before the accident at the ship site. Your eyes are both the same color, and your form is not off or mismatched anywhere."

"Truly? Then maybe Brendan's pattern replaced the base form." He was excited by the prospect of the repair, although he hoped his water horse was still the prime form. It was the puca's favorite.

"You will need to tell Grania and Brendan about this."

"Why?"

"They are now our friends, and they should know that you have accidentally acquired Brendan's form. Think how they would react if you should suddenly appear in it in front of one of them." She got to her feet and started to say something, barely opening her mouth before she vanished.

Oh boy, Dari had seen this many times before. She'd been suddenly summoned to someone in the O'Ceagan family, someone who may be dying. Her job was to arrive to give a warning or to be there at the end. Since this was the first summons since they had been on Erinnua, it was likely a warning although it could be a sudden death.

As Dari waited for her to return, he considered her request that he tell the captain. While he conceded that he understood her point, he still didn't believe it necessary. But if he were to use Brendan's construct anywhere around this area, he would be mistaken for the lad, and it would get back to him. These kinds of things always did, it seems.

Sheilan popped back in as suddenly as she had departed, a grim look on her face suggesting it had been unpleasant and unwelcome. She sighed and sank to the ground next to the puca, pulling her knees up, crossing her arms over them, and dropping her chin on top.

"That must have been bad," Dari said.

"Indeed. 'T'was Liam I was called to visit."

Liam? Dari sat up in alarm. Had something happened to him? What of the project? She easily guessed the panic in his face.

"'T'was a warning. It seemed very vague to me, but I think it has something to do with that reactor problem. There is high risk for him, it appears, and I had to warn him. I do not know if he understood what I was cautioning him about, but you will need to be alert on that excursion if it goes through still."

Dari's mouth dropped open as he stared at her. "You were sent to the ship at the station? From here?"

"No, he was at the port in a tavern."

Worse news. "You appeared in public?" The last thing she had wanted was to be seen by a large group of people. She had been trying to keep her existence here low key. Granted, they would not have seen the young woman image she wore now, but an older, middle-aged one was likely, and she looked like the washer at the ford when she was called. With her warning and wailing, she would have been quite noticeable.

"Not exactly. I appeared to him in the men's room, where thankfully, we were quite alone. Of course, I had to go through the whole warning routine and could not actually talk to him or answer his questions. He had plenty, I assure you. As will his sister when she comes to see me tomorrow."

Dari rolled his head in agitation. "Was she there, too?"

"Not at all. But you can be sure Liam contacted her afterward, and she will look into it. Mark my words on this. This is the problem of getting involved with your charges on a more personal level. They think they have special privileges."

"Ah. You are right there. Perhaps it was a mistake to make yourself known to them. Or maybe I should say ourselves since I seem to have a similar problem." Dari let his feet sink into the dirt as they sat in silence, mulling their own transgressions in this situation.

"I agree with you that I should tell Grania about my new pattern," he said at last.

"Well, then you can get in line behind me because she will be talking to me first. I tried to tell her I could not control this aspect of my duties." She looked glum.

"There is one good thing, bean sidhe. Now, you can tell the Council that you are still fulfilling your duties on this new world, and it justifies your decision to leave Earth."

Her head turned toward him as she gave a wry, little laugh. "I guess that is something, puca. Maybe it will work to my advantage. But I hope I do not have to return to Liam a second or final time. Grania and her family will not forgive me for that."

"But it wouldn't be your fault," Dari said. "You're only the messenger."

"True. But they would not see it that way." She switched forms then into her spirit ball and slipped into the soil.

"Good idea," Dari mumbled and followed suit.

*****

As predicted, Grania showed up the next morning, and although she wore a worried face, she didn't seem angry. Sheilan and Dari had settled on the grass by their tree where they recalled some old times that they'd shared together from a previous century. There were a lot of those, so pulling out these stories now and then didn't get tedious.

"A fair morning," the captain called as she came toward yhem. Her auburn hair blazed with golden highlights in the early morning sun, and she looked relaxed and casual in a simple pair of tan slacks with a gold-colored tunic.

Dari could see the dark circles under her eyes where she'd no doubt worried about Sheilan's warning to her brother through most of the night. For himself, he had to worry whether it would affect her decisions regarding their project.

"'Tis fair and gentle breezes on you," Sheilan answered her greeting, motioning to her to join them.

Choosing to face them, Grania folded herself to the ground with crossed legs. She wasted no time in getting to the point. "What did you tell Liam last night, bean sidhe? He seems confused and more than a little worried."

"As he should be," Sheilan answered. "I am but a conduit for the words, you understand, Captain. 'Tis a warning from the sidhe, who guards your family, that a death is probable within a week. Whether it comes to pass is up to the decisions Liam makes in the next few days."

"Can you be a little more specific?" she replied, her eyes flashing a spark of impatient light.

"What I said to him was, 'Take caution for danger lurks in unexpected places for your endeavor. A wrong step may prove sorrowful.' How Liam interprets that is up to him." Sheilan made no apologies. Her mission was fulfilled.

"You have to admit it's vague," Grania persisted. "Are you talking about the destruction of the ship and the reactor or is there something else that might threaten him?"

"That I cannot tell you for I have not seen the specific danger. On the ship, I knew when I faced you what threatened you and all of us, and I could see it with my own eyes. But this, no, I do not have a picture of the danger. Perhaps, if there is a second warning, I might know more."

Grania's shoulders slumped. "Well, that doesn't help a lot, Sheilan. 'Tis my decision to make if we go forward with the plans that my brothers and Dari have put together. I feel that it's important–vital even– that we correct the problem and begin the healing of the sea. Maybe this isn't the best way to go about it. Perhaps the plan has a flaw, and it's dangerous. I don't want to risk my brother's life."

"And what does your brother say about it?" Sheilan asked.

"He is mulling it over and looking at the plans again with his friend. Like me, he feels it's important and must be done. I believe that he will choose to risk his life to do it."

"As will I," Dari added, even though he had no vulnerable life to risk unless the whole pattern of corporeal forms could be erased from his essence. He hadn't quite thought about that until that very moment. No matter, it was a risk he would take.

Sheilan cast an amused look at him, thinking much the same as Dari did. However, Grania gave him an appraising look and nodded her head.

"Something a puca would risk himself for must be very important. Why is that, Dari?"

"Keep in mind that a part of my makeup is a water creature, Captain Grania. This form I wear is not my prime corporeal one, nor is it my true form. I have a keen interest in seeing the seas restored to normal. Also, as I believe it will over time affect more than the waters, and probably already has affected your plant life, it will eventually affect the humans on the planet. If Sheilan and I are to live here, we would prefer it to be a populated and Earth-like planet. I may be a trickster, but I do not desire the extinction of any of the creatures of this world."

Her lips curved into a tight smile. "I guess there is more to a puca than the legends suggest. Thank you."

"Having said all that," Sheilan said as she focused her eyes on Dari. "Is there something more you would like to tell Grania?"

"That I would like to tell?" An audible gulp escaped from his lips. "No, I would not like to tell. But I do feel I must confess something, and I trust you will be understanding, Captain."

"What is it, Dari? Have you frightened more school girls in the village?"

"I wish it were so simple. Here is how my shape changing works…" He took a deep breath and explained how his base energy stores patterns of forms that he could take and to get the pattern, he only had to sample a bit of the form. "Having said that, here is what happened yesterday. Brendan and I had a bit of an accident, and we cut each other in an eager stab for a bit of cheese. He bled on my hand, and I seemed to have acquired his pattern. So now I have –"

"Wait a minute," Grania interrupted. "You 'acquired his pattern'? Are you saying you have a sample stored of his DNA?"

Dari displayed his befuddled look. "Dee in, what?"

She laughed. "It means our genetic code, a key sequence stored in the body's cells that creates the shape and characteristics of our body. We call it our DNA map. So, if you have Brendan's, then does that mean…?"

"That I can take on the form of your brother? Yes, it does." He confessed it with a twitch of nervousness and much glancing at the ground. Would she be upset?

"Oh, my stars! That is... Well, that is quite a trick, puca. In some ways, it's pretty amazing, although I don't know how Brendan will feel about having a twin. You are going to have to tell him." Her gaze turned stern then. "And you will not go around this town or this whole planet pretending to be my brother. Is that clear?"

So much for picking up any pretty lasses in the pub. Dari nodded in agreement. He hoped Brendan would take the news as well as she had.

CHAPTER 17

Under Danger's Shadow

Two more tense days passed as Dari worried whether the plan was going to proceed before he received word via a hand-delivered message from Liam. The engineer stated, in brief words, that the plan was on track and Dari needed to notify the Ragurans that it would occur at mid-day two days hence. The team would be at the shore by the Ogham Stone about two hours after sunrise to take the shuttle out, and Dari should meet them there.

The puca decided to go out shortly after morning tea to talk to Gradifin and Alia. Together, they could get the word out to any others in the nearby area. The pair had assured him that they could keep most normal sea animals away from the zone with a simple patrol at a safe distance from the gorge. The majority of them stayed away anyway, not liking the feel of the water near the glowing light.

Once Dari reached the point where the Raguran dome was located, he changed to his water horse form, plunged in, and swam toward the occupied section where he expected he would find Alia. He sent a mental call out to her as he propelled forward to alert her that he had news and would be there shortly. After a few minutes, she acknowledged him, indicating she would meet him.

A short distance from the entrance, Dari spotted a squidie lurking behind a growth of underwater ferns and coral-like stalks.

He alerted Alia to its presence and began to move away from it, planning to pass it by without attracting its notice. He soon realized he already had its attention as he glimpsed the shift and a tentacle slipping around a rock on the seafloor. Like most equines, Dari's water horse vision was limited to what he could see from a side angle and was rather weird when compared to human eyes.

Therefore, he didn't see Alia until she appeared abruptly from nowhere and attacked the squidie with her spiked tail whipping around to cut straight into its soft body. A gush of purple filled the water around it, and Alia grabbed at the now-flailing tentacles with her clawed talons. Her short arms brought her close to the creature, but she seemed unconcerned, and in a few more moments, she yanked it from its hiding spot and hauled it out into the open. Dari realized then that it was dead. Her first strike had killed it.

Food, she sent. The hunted had become the conquering hunter.

Dari followed her back to the dome where Gradifin met them. She turned the dead squidie over to her brother's mate, and the three of them went to an empty cave to meet.

After Dari relayed the message from Liam and explained the plan, he told them that they would be setting off explosions to collapse the gorge sides inward.

Not like, Gradifin mind-spoke and the anger rang in the power of the message. *Big shakeup unsafe.*

We make safe, Dari told him. *Must do to destroy ship.*

Then Alia chimed in. *Hurt dome with undersea waves?*

Liam says no. Far enough distance from explosion. They had talked about it, but now Dari wondered if he was correct. Gradifin and Alia had cause to worry. A hard wave could do a lot of damage. *I ask them to run model again.*

They didn't understand about a simulation, so he tried to explain. *They create a model of gorge and surrounding area in their machine, and it makes test of explosions and effects from it. Your dome safe.*

They argued more. To illustrate, Dari tried to show them the image from the computer indicating the placement of the charges, and the explosions following the water flow out to their dome where it barely bumped against it. He could tell they were confused by the images, but he could not think of a way to explain a computer simulation to them when he barely understood how it worked himself.

At last, Gradifin yielded although he was still worried about the explosions. He agreed to get the word out to his people and clear the area of any stray fish or other sea life by the stated time, which he had to show to him as the sun being overhead reflecting full light through the water.

As Alia escorted him back to the dome exit, she said, *We trust you, Dari. Do not fail us.*

He nodded, unable to make a promise that he could not control. His trust had to rest in the humans.

* * * * *

By the time Dari met the shuttle on the beach, he had been fretting over how to tell Brendan about the accident. He hoped that maybe Grania had already told him.

The youngest O'Ceagan greeted him with a cheerful smile as soon as he climbed out of the shuttle. His good nature was evident and told Dari that he didn't know, but he asked anyway. "Did Captain Grania say anything to you about me?"

Brendan looked at him, a puzzled expression on his face.

"About what?"

Dari glanced around and saw that Liam and Trigg were stretching their legs and getting some readings like wind speed and other technical data, or so they said before they headed out. He pulled Brendan aside and confessed the same thing he had to his sister.

For a long, painful moment, Brendan just gawked at Dari, his mouth hanging open in surprise. Then he started laughing. "Are you kidding me, mate? That is bleeding awesome. Show me!"

"I cannot," Dari objected. "I promised the captain I would not impersonate you."

"But I want to see," he said. "If I give you permission, you can do it."

"My clothes won't fit your body," Dari hedged, reluctant to change in front of him.

"I don't believe you can do it." He challenged the puca.

"I warned you," Dari said, not stepping down from a dare, and changed into a duplicate of him, albeit stark naked.

Brendan's eyes went wide as he stared at Dari, his eyes roving from top to bottom, taking in the details. He walked around the puca, looked at his backside, then came to face him again. "You're a perfect copy of me with no flaws, no blemishes. Not even the ones where I've gotten injuries. It's amazing, Dari. If we could duplicate how you do it, we could make a fortune, but we would need to figure out a way to transfer human energy to it."

Dari quickly changed back before Liam came looking for them and pulled his clothing on again. "I can't tell you how I do it because I do not know how it works. It is just part of what I am."

He shrugged, "I know. You have to admit, though, that it would be really spectacular if we could somehow duplicate it."

About that time, Liam called them to the shuttle, and they strolled back to it as if nothing had transpired. As they climbed on board, ready to tackle this job, Dari vowed to keep a close eye on Liam so that nothing happened to him.

Within forty-five mites, they reached the location where they hovered above the underwater gorge, and Liam brought the shuttle down close to the surface. As Trigg pulled out the environment suits, he realized that the one they had brought for Dari was too large for even his harper form.

"Why don't you take on my body, Dari?" Brendan suggested. "It would fit you then."

The puca shot a sharp glance at him, annoyed that he'd brought it up.

Liam cast a questioning look at the two of them. "What's he talking about?'

Dari's shoulders slumped as he sat in one of the spare seats and related the whole bleeding story again. Brendan grinned at him like a silly fool throughout the whole ordeal. When he'd finished, Liam glanced at his brother then back to Dari.

"Is this some kind of joke, Dari? Did the two of you come up with this together?" He clearly didn't believe his tale.

"Not at all," Brendan answered. "He told me just before we got in the shuttle and even demonstrated the change. It is a perfect, and I do mean perfect, duplicate of me."

Liam sat back, his eyes growing thoughtful as he considered the possibilities of this revelation. "It might work if you change, Dari. The suit would definitely fit Brendan, so it would be fine to protect you under the water. Otherwise, we would have no way to keep you safe that close to the reactor."

Dari knew he was right about that. Even the sea dragon form succumbed to the radiation that close to the source. He couldn't go down there without protection, and this was the best bet. His harper form stood just too short to wear the larger suit.

"I have a spare set of clothes," Brendan volunteered, reaching for a bag under his seat that he offered to him. "You can change in the loo."

Dari snatched the bag from his hand and went into the tiny closet of a relief facility. Designed for short-term use, the shuttle provided just the one unit, and it only held a slim toilet and a washbasin. He took off his clothes and folded them up, then changed into Brendan's form.

As the body reflected in the metal walls, Dari noted that he was a fine-formed lad with broad, strong shoulders. When, at some point down the road, when Brendan was no longer alive, he might just honor him by making this his primary human form. He pulled on the pants and the tight-fitting shirt, tucked his clothes in the bag, then returned to the main cabin.

Liam and Trigg stared at him as soon as he came into view. "Fated fairies, if that doesn't beat the forest fool," Liam said, his expression referring to a game that the children on the planet played. Dari had seen them doing it a few times, and he still didn't understand how it worked.

"It's bleedin' eerie," Trigg said, then frowned a bit before turning his head away and back to the machine he was monitoring. Dari had a strong feeling that Trigg didn't approve of him. Not that it mattered to the puca.

"Try on the suit," Brendan urged and handed it to him. It looked like a coverall with some kind of zipper-seal at the front that he only had to step into and pull up.

Easy enough. Dari stepped into it as Brendan pulled his on as well. Then he tapped a button on the shoulder, and the seal automatically closed the suit, making a leak-proof envelope around his body, or so he informed Dari as he tapped the button on the puca's coverall. It felt snug, but comfortable, and he could move easily in it.

After locking in the position of the shuttle, Liam clambered into his suit while Trigg set up the pulley to lower them into the water. The helmets and the air tanks locked onto their backs, and they were ready to go. Trigg donned his suit last as Liam, the first down, lowered to the water. If he was worried at all about Sheilan's warning, he didn't show it.

When the lift returned, Brendan urged Dari to be the next out, then he followed him down, jumping from the ship into the water. Trigg locked the pulley in place at the bottom and slid down the cable to the water, slipping into it smoothly. They may not have done any sea swimming on Erinnua, but clearly, they all had learned how and had experience from somewhere.

Unfortunately, Dari's vast experience as a water horse did not translate as well to human form. Where he was used to flipping his tail from side to side to push himself forward, he found the pair of legs were not as effective. He watched how Brendan used an up and down wiggle with his legs held together to work his way downward in a smooth motion and tried to copy it. Taking several tries, and minutes, to get the hang of it, Dari finally managed the rhythm, but he lagged behind by several yards.

Liam made it to the top of the gorge rim well before the rest of them got there. He studied it while looking into a handheld device that showed the big hole and gave him an information readout. Through the headset built into Dari's helmet, he heard Liam's voice.

"Trigg, the readings show it a little deeper than we initially got from the scans. It may vary along the bottom. We might need to adjust the charge placements on the walls of it. Can we run a remote simulation, Bren?"

Dari turned his head to see Brendan a few feet from him. He'd pulled out one of the little computer tablets they all carried that was in a waterproof case and tapped into it. "I'm linked to the shuttle computer, Liam. I can do it from here."

"Good. Trigg, let's go down and take a look at that reactor and the engine set up. Bren, you'll want to see if you can tap into any of the ship's computers or if they are too badly destroyed to get anything."

"Will do," he replied and swam toward the main section of the ship that was about two hundred feet from the reactor.

That left Dari to take a look around the area to see if it had been cleared of all sea creatures as Gradifin had promised.

Dari swam up again and out to the rim then beyond it, looking for any indicators of fish or other marine animals in the zone. As far as he could see, the waters appeared clear. About another two hundred yards away, the puca got a peek of a figure moving around the edge and readily identified it as one of the sea dragons on patrol. He attempted to contact Alia without success. He guessed she probably was beyond his range to reach from here.

Over his headset, he heard Brendan saying, "There's still a lot of stuff left behind in the ship, personal things like trunks, statues, crosses, and all that they didn't get out before they sank the ship. There's also some navigational equipment on their bridge. I'm going to see what I can salvage of it if anything."

"Go for the data," Liam answered. "If you can access any data recording equipment, like a chip, card, or anything like that, it could provide information still once it has dried out."

"Right," Brendan's voice replied, as clear as if he'd been standing next to Dari.

"Need any help, Brendan?" the puca asked, hoping he didn't have to do anything special to be heard.

"Maybe," he replied. "Come on down, and I can put you to work."

Dari knew Brendan had gone into the main section of the ship so he swam that way and soon found himself in the sodden shell of the metal behemoth. At one point, some forms of sea life had tried to get a foothold in it leaving shells, bones, and scaly beaks behind, but nothing lived within it now. Bits and pieces of furniture and twisted metal lay scattered along the way, most looking tarnished or dull from being underwater so long. A fair amount of rust showed in some places where the metal had contained iron.

Dari looked for anything to indicate the direction he should go to find Brendan, but for the most part, the corridor didn't have places that branched. Cabin doors lined the way, most of them closed although a few had popped open when the ship crashed.

Straight ahead, he spotted a bulkhead and beyond it was a side corridor that led to another section. He took that. Within a minute, he spotted the open door to the engineering section and pushed his way through the door jamb. Holding a screwdriver, Brendan twisted and turned it as he tried to remove a section of the cabinet below a computer keyboard.

"Dari's with me," Brendan told the others when he spotted the puca. "We'll get out as much as we can from here. Did you lower the platform, Trigg?"

"Yes. It's sitting on top of the water, just below the shuttle. You can load up anything big you need to take back onto it." Trigg answered. He worked with Liam, figuring out how to shut down the core.

"How's it going there?" Brendan asked as he motioned to

Dari to come to help him. He pulled the cover off and handed it to him.

"It's tricky," Liam said. "The by-pass valve is hard to access, but I think we just about have it. If so, then this baby won't have any more fuel to keep it going."

"Let us know," Brendan replied. He reached into the cabinet and pulled out what he told Dari was a motherboard with at least twenty data pods in it.

"I don't see how those would be any good," Dari said. "The water would have destroyed them, wouldn't it?"

"Depends on if the computers and power were shut down before they sank the ship," Brendan answered. "If they were, then the pods themselves are sealed, and the data may be accessible. We won't know until we get them back to the Mo Croidhe or another computer lab." He handed Dari the board and pulled out a plastic sack from the pack he'd brought down with him. "Wrap it up, and we'll take it back to the platform."

A sudden whooshing noise burst through their headsets, then Liam's voice followed. "That's it! We've cut off the water feed to the reactor. Now we've got to get it shut down as quickly as possible. Trigg, hand me that spanner, and let's see if we can disengage the mechanism to access the controls."

Dari kept thinking he should be there with them, not off in safety with Brendan. If something were to go wrong, it would be now while they were trying to shut the thing down.

"I will take the cards up to the platform," Dari told Brendan who nodded at him, then turned his attention to another piece of equipment on the console.

Swimming as quickly as he could to the surface, Dari put the bag on the lowered platform. The clouds had begun to gather while they'd been underwater, and he felt that maybe a storm might be gathering. He didn't say anything to the others. It wouldn't help with what they were doing, and it might cause Liam to hurry and result in the mistake that would kill him. Or maybe not telling him might do it. That's the problem with knowing that the possibility is there for someone to die, but any steps you take or don't take from knowing it could be exactly what caused it.

Dari had given Gradifin his assurances that this would work and the explosions wouldn't harm the Ragurans or the other sea folk, but how could he say that when he wasn't even down there? He turned and dove into the water again, wishing for his water horse form with the powerful push in that tail.

When he made it down, Liam was propped against the housing that held the reactor and was using a mallet in one hand to pound the spanner he gripped in the other. The tool was on a large hex nut that locked the control in place. Trigg wasn't in sight.

"Can I help?" Dari asked as soon as he got close enough.

"Are you pretty strong, Dari? You are Dari, right?"

"Yes, and yes, I am strong. Probably more than Brendan." Even though he wore a duplicate of his body, the power the puca had came from inside his own spirit, and he knew he could pull from the elements to assist him.

"Okay, then help me try to turn this thing. The hammer isn't budging it."

He positioned himself above Liam and gripped the spanner just below the engineer's hands. A tight fit for him, Dari's gloved fingers barely had a hold. "Why would they use such a difficult system?"

"If the electronics failed, this system cut in and locked the controls with a hydraulic lock. The crew would have had a power tool to unlock it when they had the power fixed, and it would open easily. We don't have the tool."

Well, that made as much sense to the puca as why a maid might carry a basket of flowers to toss in a well and make a wish. He didn't try to puzzle it out, but summoned his strength and pulled a little more from what surrounded him. They pushed on the thing as hard as they could, and after feeling like his arm muscles were going to pop right out of his skin, the nut finally started to move.

"That's it," Liam said. "Don't let up now."

Digging in, Dari maintained his grip and a little niggling part of his spirit said something along the lines of why didn't you draw from the metal itself? He could have slapped his own head if his hands weren't so busy. Metal is an element, and as a sidhe, he could take molecules from anything—water, land, air, vegetation, metal. All he had to do was focus on it, and it began to break little pieces off to supply him with more molecules. After less than a minute, the fitting where the bolt held the metal grew looser allowing it to slide free.

"Got it!" Liam shouted, then reached in and turned a lever, then another one to shut the unit down. It took a moment, then it suddenly went dark.

"Good job, mate. We got the reactor off!" he said into the headset, and Dari heard a whoop come from Brendan.

"Terrific," Trigg answered. "Are you going to try to take that back to the shuttle?"

"No. It's too hard to unseat. It will be better off buried here." Liam gave Dari a thumbs up, which he took to mean they had done everything that needed doing here.

Trigg spoke again. "I have four of the explosives set, heading for another one right now, and I have one more to do after that."

"I'll give you a hand," Liam said. "Head on back to the shuttle, Dari. Are you done, Brendan?"

"Almost," he answered. "One more thing. It'll take a couple of minutes."

"Okay. Head up as soon as you can."

Liam and Dari started swimming up together. After a short time, Dari saw Brendan come out of the main cabin heading toward the surface. He was about to ask Liam if he would like him to help with the explosives when they were suddenly propelled forward and sideways through the water by a strong, undulating wave.

Chapter 18

A Plan Goes Awry

Dari spotted Liam tumbling, seeming to be out of control, and swam toward him as soon as he got his own bearings. Before he reached him, Dari realized the engineer was out cold, as the old folks used to say when someone wasn't responding, and just floating.

The puca grabbed hold of him and began pulling him toward the surface. Mid-way up, Brendan swam over, carrying a piece of equipment over one shoulder, and yanked Liam's other arm around his unencumbered one.

"I don't know what that was," Dari said through the helmet microphone.

"Something blew up," Brendan answered, a touch of worry in his voice. "I don't know what, but something in the ship triggered an explosion. Maybe there was a failsafe on the reactor that Liam missed. Let's get him to the platform. Trigg, Liam's hurt, and we're taking him up. Let's see what that little explosion did to the plan before you finish setting those charges."

Trigg acknowledged at once and said he'd head up shortly.

Between the two of them, they managed to maneuver Liam onto the platform, and Brendan pressed the button to raise it. As soon as they dragged Liam aboard the shuttle, Brendan started to unseal his brother's suit while Dari went for the medical kit. When he came back, Brendan had Liam out of the suit and was checking his pulse and counting. He took the med kit from Dari and pulled out an instrument that could give instant readings.

"I think he's okay," he said. "Just stunned. Good thing you two weren't right next to it when it blew."

With a chill, Dari realized that if he hadn't been there to help Liam free the nut, the blast probably would have killed the engineer. Just then the puca heard a mind-voice, very feeble.

Help. Need help.

As he recognized Alia's voice, a sense of dread filled him. Had the explosion reached the perimeter?

"I have to go back down," he told Brendan. "Don't let Trigg set off those charges."

"Your helmet!" Brendan called after him as he dived out of the shuttle.

Dari had removed it when he'd gone for the med kit, but he still wore the suit. No help for it now. He was in mid-air, and his human form couldn't breathe underwater. He released the molecules and returned to his sidhe form to dart into the water as the suit and clothing fell onto the surface of the sea. He hoped Brendan would haul it back up.

He set a beeline, which is a misnomer if ever he heard one–did anyone ever see a bee fly straight? Random thought aside, Dari shot like an arrow toward the perimeter in the direction of the dome.

I come, he sent to Alia.

Hurry. Just edge of hole. Gradifin hurt.

Gradifin? No, that could not be right. He was not supposed to be within the vacinity of the zone.

In a few seconds, Dari was at the edge and could see Alia leaning over the prone form of her brother. He switched to the matching sea dragon form and swam the rest of the way to her.

What happen? How he hurt?

He go in. He see light out and go into zone. Big wave throw him back into the rocks.

Dari crouched down, as much as he could, beside Gradifin, seeing multiple versions through the faceted eyes, but in all of them he was bleeding and looked terribly battered. His fins had been torn, and a jagged cut across his broad belly oozed purplish blood into the water. Already, Dari could sense predators coming toward them.

Take him back to dome, Dari said. He went to the other side to lift him from under his arms and Alia did the same on her side. She sent a request to other sea dragons to provide escort and keep the squidies and other feeders away while they got him home.

Gradifin was conscious and talked to them as they went. *I do to myself. I think safe. Sorry, Alahigra. I go to check on progress. I no trust Dari. My doing.*

She attempted to assure him that he would be all right and it was okay, but he knew he was dying. The blast had hit him full force while the rocks did all the rest of the damage. Liam and Dari had been lucky.

They got Gradifin to his cave where his mate could see him before he died, then Dari left to wait in the common area while they tended to him until he breathed his last.

After a while, Alia came to him, sorrow and anger in her movements and expression. *You say no one would be hurt. You lie. He is gone. My only family.*

I sorry, Alia. Explosion not set by us. Accident. If only –

No. No say. You no come here wearing his body. You no come back. Her hurt and fury projected in her mind-voice as well as her body language as her barbed tail flipped back and forth as if seeking a target.

Sad and dejected, Dari gave a sharp bob of his head, accepting her anger and her judgment. In a blink, he released the sea dragon form and darted away from her, a barely visible ball of light reflected in her eyes.

Dari returned to the shuttle just as Trigg climbed aboard. He zipped in just behind him and dashed to the little bathroom to change back into his young lad form and put on the clothing he'd tucked away.

When he stepped back into the shuttle cabin, relief flooded through him to see Liam sitting up in one of the seats. He seemed shaky and in pain, but at least, he was conscious and talking. Trigg was still getting out of his environment suit as he spoke.

"The charges are all placed, ready to be set off. How are you, Liam?"

"From the feel of it, I think I may have a couple of broken ribs. My whole mid-section is sore. I think Dari may have saved my life down there. If it had taken me longer to get the reactor disabled, that explosion would have killed me."

"Good job that he was there," Trigg replied. "We'll have medical check you out when we get back to town. For now, do you have new readings on that gorge, Brendan? I don't think it will affect the placement much, but let's be sure if we can."

"Right. I've run the depth change and a widening at the west end of the gorge. I've taken a real reading of the placements and added the strength of the explosives so this simulation should be accurate to what will happen."

"Let's run it," Trigg said as he sat in front of the large screen to watch. Dari moved into position behind him so he could see exactly what would happen. He owed Gradifin this much.

As the simulation ran, they saw the walls crumbling inward

on top of the ship as the explosions went off, all at one time, bringing the whole thing down in heap of shifting mud, stone, and dead vegetation. The walls would not entirely fill the gorge, but it would make a broad slope of land toward a newly-created underwater plain. Eventually, this would become the home of many new plants, fish, and other creatures.

A fitting end for the ship that destroyed so much, Dari thought. He could see no faults in the charges Trigg set, and Brendan confirmed as much as the computer evaluated the accuracy of the simulation at ninety-nine-point-eight percent.

They looked to Liam for the final go on it. He asked Brendan to repeat the recording of the simulation in slow motion, and they all watched it carefully, looking for anything that seemed amiss in it.

"How do we know there is not another explosive within the ship like that one that we triggered?" Dari asked.

"Good question," Liam answered. "Can we scan for it, Bren? Do we know enough about it to do that?"

Brendan shrugged his shoulders, "I have no idea, brother. I do know it will take a while to do it, and we need to get you to a medical facility soon."

"It won't take that long to get the readings. Then you can take me, but let's get this done while we can. I'm not dying here." Liam saw Dari wince as he said it. "What is it, Dari?"

"That unexpected explosion killed Gradifin. He thought it was safe and went into the dangerous area after he saw the reactor go down. The thing to think about now is that we have got everyone away from the zone, and if we leave and come back, we have to do that all again. But, much to my dismay, Alia does not want to see or speak to me anymore. She blames us for what happened to her brother."

Liam's expression changed to a sad, concerned face. "I am sorry, mate. We just had no idea. But it's apparent we are needing to finish this job now, so let's get those scans. If another one of those explosives is down there, we need to either defuse it or detonate it when no one's around."

As Brendan ran the scans and Trigg double-checked the calculations, Liam got painfully to his feet and stretched out on a cot that was a little too short for his tall frame. Dari sat there feeling as useless as a will-o-the-wisp on a full moon night. Then he realized something.

He dashed back into the small closet, took off his clothes again, and reverted to his little golden ball. He had refraction vision, seeing things in forms. He could go look at the ship without disturbing anything. He could pass through the walls, equipment, and anywhere he chose with no problems. He sped past Brendan, seeing his startled movement as he realized the puca was in spirit form, then Dari dove into the water again.

Pure energy moves quickly and without any hindrances through water or any other matter. It pours into between spaces and yet all the time Dari could visualize the forms in lines and curves with energy flows along them that helped him identify their function and components. He comprehended what he saw, and what he thought, as he scanned it. When he saw the remains of the destroyed reactor, Dari also got a glimpse of the device that had done it. He registered its components and went through the whole area looking for anything that matched.

He found a similar item, but upon closer inspection, decided it was not going to blow up anything even though part of it had been made from the same material. Satisfied the ship had no more explosives, Dari returned to the shuttle and told them what he'd found, or to be accurate, not found.

Liam looked pale, and Dari saw the concern on Brendan's face. "Has the bean sidhe come yet?" he asked.

"No," Liam answered shortly. "Not since the night at the pub and not today."

"We have time then." Dari knew that if Liam were close to death, Sheilan would have materialized to give warning to both of the O'Ceagan lads. His injuries may be painful, but they did not appear to be life-threatening.

Trigg shot a strange look at the two of them, and from that, Dari concluded that Liam had not told him about the other sidhe on their planet.

"So, do we blow this thing or not?" Trigg asked, tension showing in the set of his shoulders and the intent expression on his face.

"Liam?" Brendan asked, deferring to his older brother.

Opening an eye, he said, "If the two of you are satisfied that it's safe, then go ahead. I'd look myself, but I don't think I can trust my vision at the moment."

"That's it, then," Trigg said, then pressed the remote button on his tablet. "We have thirty seconds to get out here."

Brendan moved then, getting to the shuttle's controls and urging it forward into a tight circle back toward the shore.

On the bigger screen, Trigg had linked in a video camera that showed the ship and the crevice with enough detail to see the dirt crumbling loose in places where he'd disturbed it to plant the charges. On the screen, a timer counted down the seconds and all of them, excepting Liam, watched as the numbers went down until it hit zero.

Then the explosions went off, and it looked like a massive landslide into the gorge with a volcano explosion of mud shooting up in the water. Brendan slowed the shuttle and brought it about to look back at the area they'd left. The water still churned and a muddy-white color made a large irregular-shaped blemish over the sea.

After about ten minutes, the image on the screen showed the gorge more clearly, and no sign of the ship remained visible, even as more of the mud and rock continued to pour into the crevice.

"That's it," Brendan said. "It will be settling for a few days, then we'll come back to check it out. A team of experts from the water plant will begin working to clear the radiation from the water. Now, let's get my brother to the medical facility."

"Thank you," Dari said to Brendan and Trigg. He caught Liam's hand and squeezed it as he had seen humans do. "Especially to you, Liam. You'll be all right. I'll leave you here."

Then he went to the back of the ship and changed to his sidhe form out of their view and buzzed the exterior of the shuttle once before diving beneath the surface for an underwater view. In very little time, he returned to the sea dragon dome, circling around it to inspect. Relief flowed through him as he confirmed it looked the same with no damage evident anywhere. More, the Ragurans appeared calm as they swam through the city. He refrained from even attempting to contact Alia; he did not know if she would ever forgive him.

At least, they would have the chance to rebuild their former world, and he had helped to achieve that. So far as his excursions as a water horse, he knew they would be in other waters far away from here.

*****

After he returned to land and his human form, he found Sheilan to tell her they had finished. "It's up to the experts now to begin cleaning the water. I regret the loss of Gradifin. I think that in time, we might have become friends. 'Tis obvious now that I will not even have that with Alia."

"I am sorry for that, puca," Sheilan replied as they strolled along the shoreline. "I sensed you had begun to have feelings for her."

"Feelings? Not strong attachments, no. But I did like her and considered her a friend, another water life who shared that environment. Peculiar, isn't it, that a sidhe would care about any life form?"

Chuckling, the bean sidhe considered his question a moment. "I have often thought about that meself, Dari. When I first started the task eons ago, I cared little about the family I had been assigned to warn of impending death, doing my job and wandering the island when I was not needed. Since my kind is not exactly social, I had a lonely existence, and I was fortunate to strike up a friendship with a puca. You, Dari."

She paused and gazed at Dari with a look of fondness. "Somewhere along the line, I began to watch the humans more closely, and I developed a link of some sort with them, growing to care more about some of them. You could even say that my assigned clan actually became my family. I think our association with the humans, or even other creatures, changes how we view them. Our long life spans leave us too much time to be nothing more than spirits unless we interact with others. Then, when you do connect with them, you begin to care about them."

"Ah, I see your point." Dari kicked at a twisted seashell that had washed onto the shore. Not twisted in the way the Earth ones were, but in a Dali way with off angles and shapes. The result of the radiation that flooded the waters near the now-dead reactor. "I did wonder though, now that I think about it, when the explosion occurred at the ship as Liam and I were swimming to the surface, why were you not summoned to warn Liam?"

"Oh, I was. Straight to the O'Ceagan, himself, I was. The explosion should have killed Liam, so I delivered a warning wailing to the old man. I almost scared him to death in the process. I expect I will face Grania for that one." Her mouth curved into a rueful line. "If you hadn't been there, he would have died. As it was, he came very close and who knows what it might have done to you."

"Me? I am a sidhe, immortal," Dari protested.

"So we believe. It could have impacted you in other ways, wiped the patterns from your mind, changed your form or twisted it."

Surprised, Dari took a few minutes to consider Sheilan's words accepting the possibility she proposed. 'Twas true that they didn't know the limitations of their immortality. Were they truly indestructible? With a shudder through his physical form, he switched back to his energy form and darted away to ponder his existence.

EPILOGUE

A Sad Departure

On the day after Dari had helped to seal the broken ship and its once-dangerous reactor away forever, Sheilan said, "'Tis time, Dari. I can no longer avoid the inevitable. The Council summons me, and the pull is stronger each day." Seated on the ground with her legs tucked under her skirts, she petted her kitcoon friend as she talked.

"When?" Dari asked, his spirit sinking at the thought of her leaving.

"Today. This morning, I spent a the better part of an hour watching the sunrise, committing its beauty to my memory. All in all, I think it will be okay, my old friend. I have done precisely what I was fashioned to do. I trust that the Council will agree, and they will allow me to return soon. If not, then you have a choice, puca. You can stay or take the dirt route back to Earth, assuming it works properly."

"What if it doesn't?" Dari asked. Neither of them had been eager to find out, so now would be the test.

"Then it may take me considerably longer to get back to Earth if I find meself drifting in some other dimension," she said with a chuckle. "Have faith that I set up the connection properly. Perhaps I can send something back to let you know that I made it safely."

"For sure, that would be good to know. I do not want to think of you lost and drifting somewhere. Are you taking Chaka with you?"

She scratched the creature's ears and shook her head. "I couldn't do that or reduce him to energy like you and I are. Besides, he would not fare well on Earth, and with me going on to Eterien, he would be lost and alone. Perhaps you would stroke his head every now and then to remind him of me."

"Perhaps," he agreed, reaching over to pat the little beastie's head.

Sheilan gave the animal a gentle squeeze, then released it to go off into the bushes. She rose to her feet, shook the grass off her skirts then turned to him as Dari pushed himself up also.

"You take care of yourself, my friend. And try to stay out of trouble."

Dari's mouth crooked into a half-hearted smile. He couldn't promise that, but he would make an effort.

With a slight wave of farewell, the bean sidhe transformed in an instant into her spirit form. Her energy ball circled over the plot of dirt that they had brought with them that would, spirits willing, serve as a conduit to Ireland on planet Earth. From there, she would use another soil portal to go to Eterien.

Dari choked up as he realized he might not see her again. They had shared many centuries as friends and to be without her scared him more than he could admit. "I would gladly go with you."

Her mind touched his. *Not this time, old friend. I will be back as soon as I can. Be safe.*

"Safe home," Dari whispered as her energy darted into the ground at his feet and a golden glow filled it for a moment before she vanished. After that, he could detect no more trace of her. How long would it take? Would she be in Ireland already or was she in transit for a time? As far as they knew, no sidhe had used a soil portal from deep space even though one had traveled from Mars.

When at least thirty or forty minutes had passed, Dari changed forms and zipped into the dirt to feel its familiarity and seek any trace of Sheilan's passage. In a moment of panic, he worried what he would do if she did not return. How would he ever know if she made it or not? Or if she had made it and the Council had barred her return? How would he know if he could ever get back?

Uncomfortable in the usually comforting soil, Dari returned to his lad form and sat under the nearby tree as he gazed at the plot of dirt. He could be stuck here forever or forced to find a spaceship to travel back to Earth. That frightened him. He was just a puca, full of pranks and silly ideas, but he wasn't all that good at planning things.

But then, as he reminded himself he'd just helped to right a problem on this world, so maybe he could figure things out better than he thought he could, a luscious-looking Irish turnip popped out of the dirt. Whooping with excitement, Dari snatched it up. Sheilan had sent a snack.

The End

From the Author: If you enjoyed this book, please consider leaving a review at the bookseller's web site. Reviews help others to find books they might enjoy as well as giving me a creative boost knowing that you took the time to review. Thanks!

About the Author

A sometimes musician, sporadic artist, occasional poet, and obsessed writer, Lillian Wolfe has spent most of her life writing. From fan fiction to short stories, novels, training manuals, newsletters, and other documentation, she has constantly been putting words on paper or a computer screen. She is, in fact, extremely grateful for the invention of the computer because using a manual typewriter is tedious. While she loves all types of fiction, her favorites are fantasy and mystery novels.

Lillian shares her home in northern Nevada with her best friend for the past thirty-odd years and three feisty felines. She is a member of the High Sierra Writers Group and the Fiction Writers Group.

You can contact Lillian through her web site:
http://www.lillianwolfe.me/loft/
and/or at her Facebook Page:
https://www.facebook.com/LilliansLoft

Other Books by This Author

O'Ceagan Saga

O'Ceagan's Legacy

Funeral Singer Series

A Song for Marielle

A Song for Menafee

A Song of Betrayal

A Song of Forgiveness

A Song of Redemption

Time Threads Series

Time Walker – *coming in May, 2019*

www.ingramcontent.com/pod-product-compliance
Lightning Source LLC
LaVergne TN
LVHW090948080826
845145LV00003B/930

* 9 7 8 1 9 4 2 6 2 2 2 0 8 *